SCABMUGGERS

SCABMUGGERS

A NOVEL

YVONNE MARTINEZ

SHE WRITES PRESS

Copyright © 2025 Yvonne Martinez

All rights reserved. No part of this publication may be reproduced, stored in a retrieval system, or transmitted in any form or by any means, electronic, mechanical, photocopying, recording, or otherwise, except for brief quotations in reviews, educational works, or other uses permitted by copyright law.

Published in 2025 by
She Writes Press, an imprint of The Stable Book Group

32 Court Street, Suite 2109
Brooklyn, NY 11201
https://shewritespress.com
Library of Congress Control Number: 2025909821
ISBN: 978-1-64742-966-9
eISBN: 978-1-64742-967-6

Interior Designer: Kiran Spees

Printed in the United States

This is a work of fiction. Names, characters, places, and incidents are either products of the author's imagination or are used fictitiously. Any resemblance to actual persons, living or dead, is purely coincidental.

No part of this publication may be used to train generative artificial intelligence (AI) models. The publisher and author reserve all rights related to the use of this content in machine learning.

All company and product names mentioned in this book may be trademarks or registered trademarks of their respective owners. They are used for identification purposes only and do not imply endorsement or affiliation.

Based on a true story

Dedicated to
Union Women who dare to fight the good fight
wherever it takes them.

CONTENTS

1: Winter Is Coming. Winter Is Here. 1

2: Radcliffe Hall 8

3: Reasonable Guys. 11

4: Bet? Bet. 15

5: Cultural Exchange 26

6: Mill Girls 32

7: This Is Our Shot 37

8: Class Speaker 46

9: The Great Cannoli Lockout 52

10: Harvard Union Women 65

11: The Plaque. 69

12: Lightning Struck the Garbage Truck. 76

13: Just Say Yes 78

14: Shake Your Tail Feathers 80

15: That's Not Happening Here. 85

16: Legal Seafood 88

17: Pennies Everywhere. 91

18: Where Is It?. 93

19: Step by Step. 96

AUTHOR'S NOTE

Although this book exposes serious conflicts within the labor movement, I have always fought for unions and union democracy.

1 WINTER IS COMING. WINTER IS HERE.

I was raised by felons until I made my First Communion. My grandmother sat me between her legs and twisted my hair into the ringlets capped under my veil. She loved Shirley Temple. Our picture in front of Our Lady of Guadalupe Catholic Church in Salt Lake shows my grandmother in a black swing coat, matching heels, and a wide smile.

I studied my *Baltimore Catechism* while she and her sister sex workers busted up Salt Lake taverns to run out scabs. An original scabmugger, she knew how to leverage a boss. Scabmuggers were neighborhood and community women, overall strike enforcers who had ways of "persuading" scabs not to cross picket lines.

In the spirit of my scabmugger grandmother's example, I became an activist myself. Mid-career as a labor negotiator/organizer, I was awarded the prestigious Jerry Wurf Fellowship to attend the Harvard Trade Union Program, an executive program at Harvard University for labor leaders. Jerry Wurf was one of few white men to support a Black-led strike, the Memphis sanitation strike. The strike that the Reverend Dr. Martin Luther King went to support when he was killed. That was the mantle I wore.

Heavy snow stuck like caps around the gold and teal domes of Harvard's dorms. Sidewalks were sheets of black ice. I pulled a bulky hand-knitted wool scarf tight around my face and wore men's black work boots that weighed my feet down and anchored me in the snow.

For a counterweight, I carried a black leather backpack full of books. My classmate Ana's long black hair gathered snow like a waterfall. She wore a wool pleated skirt over thick cable-knit black stockings and black shearling boots, her hands tight in a muff. We met at the footbridge, got to know each other the old-fashioned way, face-to-face, organizer to organizer. It was 1994; there were no devices.

"Come on," I said. "We don't want to be late."

"I'm waiting for everyone else to get here. You go ahead."

"We're here now. Let's go." I pulled her elbow. "C'mon."

Under the hundred-year-old footbridge that connected our dorms to the campus ran the ice brick Charles River. Naked trees dotted the edges, bent over, heavy with ice.

I held my hand out to her. "Can you believe this? Thirty trade unionists from all over the world, and where do they house us? At the Harvard Business School, the citadel of capitalism, right inside the belly of the beast."

Ana took my hand.

"It's a sheet of ice. We'll never get across."

"Hold on, let's hug the bridge wall."

We made it to the top of the footbridge. I kicked the snow off my boots.

"Okay, now all we gotta do is make it down."

"We'll be late for our first day at Harvard."

"We won't be late by much. Everybody's got to get over this damn bridge. It's just speeches and mingling tonight. It'll be different for class in the morning."

Holding on to each other, we slid down, hit the bottom, and fell into the snow. Helping each other up, we dusted off snow and walked to the crosswalk. I saw something shiny in the snow.

"Look, a penny."

I picked it up and put it into Ana's hand. She wrapped her fingers around it.

WINTER IS COMING. WINTER IS HERE. 3

"A good sign. I'm amazed you could find anything in this blizzard. It's one of the worst nor'easters we've ever had."

Ana put the penny back in my hand, catching my glance.

"You know, I'm not as political as you are. I mean, I'm no big-time union rep or president of a union like you guys all are. I'm just a secretary for a teachers' union."

"Nobody's just a secretary."

"I don't have degrees and titles."

"A lot of us don't either."

"You know what I mean. I don't even represent anyone."

"Leaders don't always have titles. Some of the most effective and powerful shop floor leaders I've known pushed a mop and broom. Your union sent you here for a reason. Trust that. You belong here just as much as the rest of us do. Where are you from, anyway?"

"We're from Rhode Island. My dad was connected, you know, a 'made' man. I was driven to school every day in an armored car with a driver. I didn't want that life, so I got out. That's how I ended up at the teachers' union." She paused. "I don't know why I'm telling you this."

"Wow! That's a story. Do you miss your family?"

"I still see them, but I'm not part of their world and they have respected that. What about you? Where do you come from?"

"I'm a fourth-generation Afro-Mexican from Utah, not a Mormon, a Catholic in a Mormon state," I said. "My grandparents raised me till I was seven. My grandfather was a kingpin in the Utah weed trade in the forties. He and my great-grandmother got caught up in a sting. They did time, my grandfather at McNeil Island and my great-grandmother at Walla Walla State Pen."

"Wow, so we both come from outlaws of some sort."

"Yup, yet somehow they made a way out of no way and we're here now because of it. Both of us in this underdog fight."

Ana pulled her muff in closer.

"I'd say that evens us out a little."

"I'd say it does."

We arrived for the evening's welcome at the Harvard Faculty Club. Wainscoting, footpath-grooved oriental carpets, old money, worn yet elegant furnishings. Ana and I entered the cloakroom to remove our coats, boots, and scarves. Jack, a burly, balding, red-faced Australian, was already there, wearing a tight-fitting double-breasted suit and a tropical-print tie. So was Aaron, a tall African American bodybuilder wearing a short black leather jacket, blue jeans, and leather boots. We took off our coats, caked snow falling in chunks around us, and sat on a bench to remove our boots.

Ana slid over to make room for Aaron as he unloaded his books. She whispered to me. "We weren't supposed to bring our books tonight, were we? Were we supposed to read everything before we got here?"

Aaron dropped his glove near Ana's foot. She reached down to pick it up. Taking her hand, Aaron stopped her and picked up the glove himself. "I wouldn't worry about it," he said.

Ana moved away from Aaron, so close to me we were hip to hip on the bench.

"The glove? Oh! I'm not."

"No, the reading, I wouldn't worry about it."

Ana whispered to me, "I just wonder if I'll keep up."

"Ana, stop. You'll be fine," I said.

Jack eyed Ana like he could see through all her layers to below her sweater, slip, and bra. He stared at Ana, then turned to nod to Aaron. "A lot of cold and lonely nights, I suspect—aye, Aaron? In need of some late-night company, perhaps."

Not this again, I thought. *Not here!*

At dusk a bed of snow covered the Harvard Faculty Club. The paned glass windows almost closed out any outside light. Elise Henri, the program director, gavel in hand, took the podium. She wore a standard-issue beige suit, perfunctory, an obligatory nod to convention.

WINTER IS COMING. WINTER IS HERE.

"On behalf of Harvard University, I welcome you to the annual Harvard Trade Union Program. Thirty of you have come from all over the United States and five countries. You have been selected by your unions because you are leaders who can make a difference in the lives of working men and women. The very life of the labor movement is at stake. In the next sixteen weeks, you will change and be changed by many events. How you fare here will matter."

Speech over, I sat at my table and worked on my pie. Aussie Liz was tall and wore square, black-rimmed glasses, men's draped pants, and a sport coat. She was a leader of the New South Wales Teachers Federation.

"Liz Marie, mate," she said in her introduction to me.

"Pleasure to meet you," I said. "Here, have a seat."

We sat in earshot of Jack and Kirk, a tall, towheaded Midwesterner. Jack gestured with his drink to Ana and Aaron.

"What do you make of that? Looks like he's got a hard-on for the secretary."

Kirk shook his head.

"Never happen."

Jack took a sip of his drink. "Don't be so sure, mate. Wogs in this country don't stay in their cages anymore. Not like back home where we've managed to sequester ours to the Outback."

Kirk leaned back. "Wogs? Is that like a wop?"

"No, it's our all-purpose term for non-whites."

Kirk moved in closer. "Better watch how you use that here."

Liz and I looked at each other. "Can you believe this bullshit?" I said. "Indeed, mate."

Jack took another sip. "It's just between us, mate. Besides, it's up to you blokes if you want wogs after your women."

Kirk held his beer up to his lips. "It's going to be a long, cold sixteen weeks, buddy. Twenty-four guys, just six women, and two of the women don't count."

6 SCABMUGGERS

Jack and Kirk looked over at us.

"Don't look now, mate. It's about to get better," Liz said.

"Like I said, those two don't count, unless you're into converting queers and taming Amazons," Kirk said.

"Lizzie, yeah, she's our poofta teacher," Jack said.

"A what?" I asked.

Jack almost finished his drink. "Poofta—our word for queer."

"Poofta? Huh. Whatever."

Jack pointed to me. "What about the other one? Looks like she might be outside the free-trade zone."

"Oh, the Latin-flavor feminist? Okay, if you like missionary work," Kirk said.

"Looks like Elise has got a little of everything here," Jack said.

"Yeah, a regular United Nations. Japan, South Africa," Kirk said.

"Quebec, Australia, and various shades of Americans including wogs, if you will. Hey listen, don't you worry about the secretary, we'll see to it that she gets plenty of opportunities to make a real choice. Consider it a Buy American campaign." Jack finished his drink.

As Liz and I walked past them, Jack stopped us. "Liz, any luck finding the newspaper from home?"

Liz gave him a short-breathed, emphatic no.

"Right," he said. "I'm told there's a kiosk not far from here on the way to class in the morning. First one in brings it in?"

She gave him a shorter-breathed answer. "Won't be you on a regular basis, I'll bet."

Jack's lips went flat. "Lizzie, be kind."

Liz left, and I started to walk away. Jack stopped me. "Jack Smith, Australian Rail Workers Federation, general secretary."

"Simone Arroyo, public sector, Seattle, Washington."

Jack circled his glass under my nose. "Can I get you a glass of wine?"

WINTER IS COMING. WINTER IS HERE.

I looked up and down at Jack's tropical tie. "No, thank you. I don't drink."

Jack ran his fingers up and down his tie. "I used to be somewhat of a chardonnay socialist myself. Now I just drink."

"Oh, a fair-weather socialist?"

Jack twisted his empty wineglass.

"Face it, mate, that lot lost, Jack said."

"The battle's not over yet. Your compatriot Harry Bridges was a dyed-in-the-wool Red, led the ILWU in the historic San Francisco General Strike, forever changing the lives of dockworkers, if not the labor movement. He organized wall-to-wall whites and wogs of all stripes alike, and no doubt pooftas too. In his view labor was labor. He didn't make distinctions like the waterfront bosses did. That's how he beat them."

Jack twisted his wineglass between his fingers. "Commie bloke, may he rest in peace."

I left him standing there with his empty glass.

2 RADCLIFFE HALL

The next morning before class, I stood on a street corner in snow that cut like ice. I held a map under the dim light of an old streetlamp, turned it, and changed direction. I dragged my boots through the snow past one ancient New England church and then stopped in front of another. I walked up the church footpath to the huge, thick, dark wood–planked and wrought iron–bracketed door, opened it, and walked down to a spare basement room. I could see my breath in the cold as I took a seat on a folded chair among a circle of women. The women ranged in age from young adult to elderly. Padded down in wool scarves, shawls, gloves, and blankets, they nodded a welcome. I opened my purse to pull out a tissue to wipe my red, dripping nose and pennies fell out onto my lap. I joined in.

"God grant me the serenity to accept the things I cannot change, the courage to change the things I can, and the wisdom to know the difference."

Meeting over, I slogged my way to campus and met my classmates at Radcliffe Hall for our first day of class. The walls were covered with embossed burgundy brocade wallpaper above the wainscoting. There were curved paned glass transoms on top of the doors, the glass fanning out like a spiderweb. The floors were wide dark brown wood planks. Crown molding, pillars, and carved molding framed the room. Curved wood and spindle banisters led up polished oak

RADCLIFFE HALL

stairs. Brass sconces lit it all up with ceilings higher than any I had ever seen. Yankee New England to be sure.

John Dunlop, a Harvard professor in his seventies, wore a bow tie and an ancient shiny blue suit. He scribbled something on the chalkboard and turned to address us.

"May I have your attention, please?"

He held a pointer up like he was about to conduct a symphony and waited with a Hitchcock half-eyelid stare.

"Please limit your comments to the assigned readings and to areas about which you have direct knowledge. I am not interested in hearsay regurgitations of events with which you have no firsthand experience. You have been selected out of thousands by your respective unions to be here, so it is presumed that you have some ability to comprehend complex ideas. It is also assumed that you have some ability to cogently express your thoughts, such as you may have any, on the subjects covered in the readings. Nothing more."

At the time, I wasn't sure what to make of this. Was this discourse a relic of post–World War II industrial unionism? Had class warfare gotten institutionalized into economic department colloquy? I learned later that Dunlop was the old guard academic don of labor studies at Harvard. The executive program I attended was his creation. In setting it up the way they did, like a "reality" survival game, I wonder how much thought was given to the participants in the experiment they created. Why was it okay to set up abuse? I later learned that every class was set up solve some kind of crisis.

Heads down, we took notes, looked sideways at each other. No one moved to break the cold between us except Palmer, a short, portly Minnesotan with wavy blond hair. His hand went up. In an ill-fitting nondescript suit and tie that appeared to be choking him, his unwilling effort to conform to convention, he waited to be called on. We waited for an anvil to fall on his head.

"Um . . . Professor Dunlop, sir, Palmer Winston here, Newspaper Guild. Could you help us understand what's on the board?"

Dunlop tapped his pointer in his hand.

"Young man, surely your many years in the newspaper industry have not caused you blindness."

Dunlop walked over, tapped the blackboard with the pointer, and turned to Palmer.

"Nor, I trust, has your considerable skill at deciphering the printed word rendered you inept upon your arrival here. Shall we try again?"

Dunlop scribbled something else unintelligible on the blackboard. His chalk broke, and white pieces fell to the floor. Some of us tried to take notes; others just stared. The Japanese students typed furiously into their handheld PC translation devices. I whispered to Ana and Liz.

"This is like the *Paper Chase* movie. Is this guy real?"

After class Ana and I ran up the massive narrow stairs to the gray concrete gym with its floor-to-ceiling arched windows. Aaron showed up as we entered. I turned to Ana.

"Do you want me to wait?"

"No, I'll meet you inside."

3 REASONABLE GUYS

The Harvard Law School dorms were mini–furnished apartments with high ceilings and tall windows. Light fell in like snowfall. A tweed Berber carpet laid out the room under a gray flannel sofa and matching chair next to a dark wood coffee table. In the small kitchen were a table and chairs for four. Next to the full-size bed in the bedroom were a desk, lamps, and bookshelves. From a window above the desk, I watched the yard below and the different textures of snow as it fell. This was where I put my back-pack down, where I studied and wrote, safe from any storm outside.

Ana and I invited Liz to my dorm. Ana's dorm was across the hall. We gathered around the coffee table. Ana cut the pizza, put it on paper plates, and handed us each a slice.

"Thanks for inviting me, mates. I hardly see my roommate. It's nice to get more acquainted."

I took a sip of my soda. "We're glad you could come."

Liz grabbed a napkin. "By the way, I've been hearing some interesting things about male-female interactions in class."

I took another sip. "You mean more than the usual pompous speechifying?"

"Yes, well more than that, mate. I thought maybe that's why you invited me here."

"Like what?"

"Our female classmates are being propositioned by some of the blokes in class."

Ana cut more pizza, offering it to Liz. "Can we talk about this without naming names?"

I took a bite and looked at both of them. "What? They're what? Talk about what?"

Ana cut the pizza into smaller slivers. "I'm not sure this is a good idea."

Liz took another slice. "Go ahead, Ana. It's okay."

"I don't know if we should be talking about this."

Liz put her pizza down. "If you don't tell her, I will."

I took a skinny slice of pizza. "What? Tell me what?"

"She's being stalked. He waits after class, insinuates himself upon her. Shows up at her dorm. Calls at night."

"Oh my god, Ana. Who?"

I hope this isn't true, but here it is again, I thought.

"She's not saying."

"Is this true? Is what Liz is saying true?"

Ana nodded.

This is all so typical, so pedestrian. I came here to knit, read, and think. I came here unarmed, having left my weapons at home. Never did I imagine I would need them here. They're targeting Ana because they think she's weak because she's a secretary. Easy prey.

"Look, that's all right, mate; it's not your fault. Is it?"

Liz turned to me. "I know why they don't want me. How did you manage to escape the honor?"

We laughed.

"Beats the hell out of me. Not the right flavor, I suppose."

Ana kept cutting the pizza. "It's not that. They're afraid of you."

"What did I ever do to them?"

"Nothing. Face it, mate, you speak up in class and know what you're talking about. It's enough to send these white bully boys running."

I put down my skinny slice of pizza while Ana cut more.

"Ya know, this is bullshit," I said.

REASONABLE GUYS

"I agree, mate," Liz said.

"This can't be allowed to go on."

"Yes, but what can we do about it?" Ana asked.

"Mates, I believe we have no other recourse but to go to Elise with the information we do have."

Ana chopped up the remaining pizza.

"Take it easy, Ana," I said.

Ana put the knife down. "Who's going?"

Liz wadded up her napkin and threw it on her paper plate.

"Looks like a job for the resident dyke and radical feminist."

Ana folded the pizza box. "No names, please. I don't want to get anyone kicked out."

I gathered up all the pizza bits. "Yes, Ana, no names. And we've got to do more than just go to Elise. Let's reach out to our sisters and our male classmates. You know, the semi-decent ones, the reasonable ones, talk to them about what's going on and ask for their support."

Liz opened a soda. "Right, mate—a Reasonable Guys Caucus? I'm sure there must be a few decent blokes in the bunch. Good idea. Let's make a list."

We tore up napkins and listed all the guys we thought might support us based on our limited knowledge of them. We made lists for ourselves and for Debbie, my housemate who was away. Our other two women classmates, Cleo and Mindy, were MIA.

Liz finished her soda. "Once we go to Elise, word is going to get around fast. We've got to get to these lists right away."

✳ ✳

Liz and I kicked snow off our boots on our way up the steps to Elise's office. Elise showed us to two chairs in front of her desk and moved stacks over to get a clear view of us.

"You appear to be some kind of delegation."

I folded my coat in my lap. "We are, of sorts."

Liz wiped the fog off her glasses. "We have a somewhat delicate matter to bring to your attention. I'm sure we can rely on your discretion and your assistance."

Elise widened the space between her stacks. "By all means."

Outside Elise's window, a clock hung on a tall, narrow pointed roof building. Clock hands had moved by a half hour when we put our coats on to leave.

Liz reached her hand through the stacks to Elise. "Thanks for seeing us."

Elise moved around her desk and stacks to shake it, then said, "I will not tolerate any untoward behavior against any member of this class. However, I must have more information in order to intervene directly."

I pulled on my gloves. "We've told you all we can."

Elise walked us out. "Aside from reviewing the standard policy, you realize there is little more I can do unless you give me names."

Liz buttoned her coat. "We cannot."

"Very well then, when you are at liberty to share more information, please call my office."

As we suspected, once we went to Elise, word of the Reasonable Guys Caucus spread in one-on-one meetings between the women organizers and the men, and the goal of reaching out to the Reasonable Guys started having results. Outside the classroom at a coffee kiosk, students milled around small tables, clustering together like a hive, grouping and regrouping.

4 BET? BET.

One of the first names on our Reasonable Guys list was Palmer. After watching him in action with petrified forest Professor Dunlop, we knew we needed him on our side. Liz and I pulled him over to a corner of the enclosed lobby area outside the classroom where the coffee kiosk was and sat at a table behind the kiosk where no one could see us.

"Sure I'll help," he said. "Where do I sign?"

Liz checked him off the list. "Can you talk to some of the other guys too?" I said.

"Yeah, sure, who do you got?" He took names and folded his list into his pocket and moved in closer.

"Wait till I tell you what I overheard on the way home the other day," he said. "Not that far ahead of me, Kirk and Jack were walking together, and Jack started in: 'Your roommate Aaron making any headway with the secretary?' he asked.

"Kirk said, 'Still hasn't happened. Not gonna happen.'

"'Bet?' Jack said.

"Kirk confirmed the bet and then explained how Aaron got here. Apparently, he scabbed the Black Firefighters Caucus of the National Firefighters Association to get here.

"'What?' Jack said. I almost said, 'What?' out loud too.

"Kirk went on to explain. 'Yeah, the Black Firefighters Caucus put demands on the National Firefighters Association to push for pro-

15

motions and hiring for Black firefighters at fire stations around the country. Aaron broke ranks with them, said he didn't need affirmative action.'"

I put my hand on Palmer's shoulder. "He said that?"

"Yes, he did. Told them it diminished him and his abilities, that it made everybody think he was given a break he didn't want or need."

Liz shook her head.

Palmer went on. "Any promotion he got was on his own merit. The National Firefighters Association sent him here as a reward."

Liz and I just looked at each other. "A regular Clarence Thomas," I said.

"That's not all," Palmer said. "Kirk said the Black firefighters put glass in his boots."

"What?" Liz and I said in unison.

"Yeah, his own people," Palmer replied, before resuming his story.

"Then Jack jumped in," Palmer said. "'Yeah, mate,' he said. 'So, let's make it interesting. Let him think if he gets the secretary, he's in with the rest of the blokes. If he gets kicked out, oh well, too bad, bye-bye, and we can demand justice for a so-called 'brother.''

"They slapped hands and laughed. I turned the corner and left."

The three of us sat there in our corner behind the coffee kiosk feeling, to use Liz's word, gobsmacked. Literally, our gobs were smacked, our tattered napkin lists in front of us.

Debbie, my roommate, a New Englander with a South Boston townie accent so thick I could hardly understand her, had joined the fight and came over to us. We all shared lists, and then Palmer and Liz left.

"Looks good," I said. "Where's Ana?"

"I haven't seen her this morning, and I don't think she's doing her list," Debbie said.

"What's going on with her? This isn't like her. We've got to get her people covered, now more than ever."

"I'll get her list from her and do it myself if I have to," Debbie said.

"Okay."

Later, Ana told me why.

In the dormitory laundry room that morning, she'd taken her clothes out of the dryer and reached halfway into the dryer drum to look for something. Aaron walked in while her back was to the dryer door and held up a pair of women's underpants.

"Looking for these?"

Ana turned and slammed the dryer door against the wall. "Where did you get those?"

"I came in early to do laundry. They were in the dryer."

"How did you know they were mine?"

"I didn't, until now."

Ana pushed the dryer door against him and took her underpants, grabbed the rest of her stuff, and left.

We dragged ourselves away from the one-on-one coffee kiosk conversations to the classroom and sat amid a buzz of talking and books hitting the desks. Jack and Kirk talked with Dick, a burly mustachioed fireman. He loved his Rolex and pulled his sleeve back to refer to it often. A reminder, in his mind, that his time was more precious than everyone else's, he stroked it as he sneered at the women and Blacks in class.

Huddled with Dick and Kirk, Jack surveyed the room.

"Something's up. The feminazis have been chatting up the blokes."

Kirk opened a book like he was interested.

"I got asked for support from the women. Didn't you, Jack?"

"How did you rate?"

"They think I'm a reasonable guy."

Dick moved closer to them.

"Yeah, well, word is that Elise is going to lower the boom on whoever's been chasing tail in the class."

Jack pointed to Liz and me.

"It's not about tail, dolts. It's them. That lot is trying to run the class and tell us what to do."

Dick rubbed his Rolex. "They can't tell us what to do."

"If Elise gets it in her head that some of us are too friendly with the sheilas, she could put us out."

"Elise wouldn't do that."

"Like hell she wouldn't."

Elise pounded the gavel.

"Before we get to business items, I have a question for you. Why do you think Harvard University has this school for labor leaders? Why would the most prestigious university in the world care about the labor movement? Clearly, it doesn't want your money, because you don't have any. It's not your brilliant minds, because notwithstanding your brilliance, the minds here aren't all that brilliant. No, so, what does Harvard want?"

Heads shifted side to side. It was riddle time again.

"It wants to know who and what you know. It wants contacts in your world; it wants access to leadership. More important than money to Harvard, because it has plenty of it, is access to power."

We looked at each other like *Who, us?*

"Moving on. First business item, if your rooms are too cold, come see me. It's been unseasonably cold and we may have to find you other accommodations."

Groans.

"Secondly, now listen carefully, I said listen carefully."

Gavel pounded.

"It has come to my attention that there has been unwanted attention directed toward female members of this class. Let me repeat, unwanted attention."

Jack was up on his feet. "Hold on, Elise, will you please elaborate? Has there been a complaint?"

BET? BET.

19

Elise tapped the gavel in her hand with a "get real" look on her face.

"I will not publicly discuss matters brought to me in confidence. A confidence you all enjoy and that it is my duty to protect. I reiterate, however, that any unwanted conduct of a sexual nature toward any member of this class will not be tolerated."

Collective muttering ensued.

Jack turned to the class, then back to Elise. "How can we possibly know what you're talking about? Are we to refrain from discussing anything with our female classmates? How are we to know what attention is unwanted?"

Elise tapped the gavel in her palm. "Glad you asked, Jack. The short answer is this: Your female colleagues will set the limits on your irresistible charm, should you choose to visit it upon them."

The class laughed.

That's right, asshole, I thought. *We decide that, not you.*

"The long answer is in this handout where the university, in Harvard's inimitable style, has spelled out for you exactly what behavior is out of bounds."

Several hands went up as the handout was passed around.

"I knew there would be questions. I invite you to read the policy and decide whether you wish to take class time or personal time for questions and answers. For now, Jim Green is here for the labor history section. I will end this discussion and begin again when and how you collectively decide to proceed. Jim."

I reached over to Liz and Debbie. "I can't believe she's going to take a dive and let the class decide if the policies should be discussed."

I put down my knitting and stood. "I don't think we should leave this discussion optional. The class as a whole should be required to review these policies."

Elise pounded the gavel on the lectern. "I am not going take up any more class time to discuss when and whether to discuss these policies. That's your decision."

20 SCABMUGGERS

I motioned to the women. "Elise, we're outnumbered here."

Men in the back row muttered louder. I looked to Ana, who sat up straight and faced forward. Elise said nothing, turned the lectern over to Jim, and left.

Jim Green, a white-haired, middle-aged history professor, wore a V-necked button-front cardigan and pleated chinos.

"Today's reading was about Ludlow. Who can tell me what happened?"

Still standing as I watched Elise leave, I turned to Jim.

"What happened? I'll tell you what happened. Striking miners, their wives and children were mowed down by machine guns. One of the first times machine guns were used. Tested on working people."

Jim pointed to the images on the wall. The images showed miners' families in tents at a campground.

"The miners were kicked out of the mining companies' quarters during the strike and they created a makeshift tent colony. And yes, the massacre was horrific, and yes, many were killed. But what was going on? What led up to the massacre?"

Jack stood. "Jim, if I may, I'd like to make a brief announcement before you get too far into your lecture."

Jim's back was to the images on the wall. "Okay, but make it short."

Jack turned to face the class. "We'd like to propose a meeting during the morning break to work things out in class, among ourselves, without Elise or any of the university bosses involved."

I faced Jack. "What's the point of that, Jack? You heard Elise. We have rules. Just read and follow them."

Dick stood up next to Jack. "Jack's right, we don't need the boss in here. We can work this out among ourselves."

Jim tapped his pointer on the lectern. "You guys work out what you need to work out during your break. It's time to get back to the lecture. This room is available to you during the morning break if you want it."

BET? BET.

Jack turned to survey the class before he sat down. "The meeting is happening for everyone."

More scenes on the wall showed Ludlow. Black, white, immigrant miners and their families in the doorways of their makeshift tents. Jim turned off the light to show more images of Ludlow including the pit where the miners hid women and children, including a pregnant woman. I stood in the dark and pointed. "That's it. That's the pit where the mine's owner, John D. Rockefeller Jr., burned women and children to death."

I sat back down with Debbie, Liz and Ana. They put their hands on my shoulders. In the dark a note was passed to us. It said: *Give us the name, we'll deal with it.*

We looked up to see Dick and Kirk flex their fists. I tore up the note in front of them. Liz leaned over to me.

"That's right, mate, hand over a Black man to a mob, not on my life."

Break time took place precisely on the minute. Declan O'Hara, a middle-aged Irishman from New York, stood to face the class.

"Now, I don't know exactly what's going on, but I know that we have to try to get along. The sisters have come to me for support and I have pledged it to them. I don't believe there is a man in this room who would hurt a woman."

Jack was on his feet. "Hurt what woman? As far as we know this could be some kind of witch hunt. Nobody has said anything about anything specific so far."

Denny, a medium-framed, bespectacled Black legal worker from the South African miners' union, stood.

"Clearly, if there is evidence of wrongdoing, those bringing charges must feel free to bring them forward. I believe we must allow Elise to conduct a class discussion so that we may be aware of the acceptable parameters of classroom behavior and appropriate channels of redress if there are violations."

Palmer stood up next to Denny. "I agree. Some of us have been approached by the sisters, so something's going on."

Liz turned to face Jack. "Look, mate, what's the mystery here? We're not yet through the second week and there are problems already. All we ask for is respect and civility."

Anthony Gleason, a middle-aged Australian with bearded black hair, stood. "Yeah, right, mates. What's the matter, ey? The sisters just want to be left alone. Got it? I don't think there's a man here who can't respect that."

Behind Anthony stood Claude, a tall, dark-haired Quebecois. "We're trade unionists, for god's sake. Let's behave like trade unionists. Let the sisters speak."

Denny, Anthony, Palmer, and Claude, a consolidation of support, had created a noticeable shift.

Jack stood. "All we're asking is that any matter be resolved here amongst ourselves, without the bosses."

Ana clutched her hands in her lap.

Liz and I conferred. I stood to speak and found myself sounding like a labor hack as I held forth. "We appreciate the words of support and solidarity offered by all our trade union brothers here, truly we do. We recognize and commend our brothers who have already stepped forward. We hope we can count on the rest of our brothers as well. However, we also wish it to be known that sexual harassment is a violation of university policy and a violation of the law. No matter what is worked out here or anywhere else, we reserve the right to bring any issue, any claim, any violation to any authority we deem appropriate, to Elise, to the university, the police, to whoever."

The red on Jack's face turned to splotches. "What? By what authority?"

Ana stood up. "Jim's outside. It's past time."

Jim opened the door and pointed to his watch.

Jack faced the room. "Hold on, we can't leave it this way."

BET? BET. 23

Dick walked over to Jim. "Jim, can you give us just a little more time?"

Jim looked around. "Okay, five minutes, but that's it."

Jack stared directly at me. I met his stare. "Like I said, Jack, we don't need anybody's permission to report a violation of the law or to bring forward any claim that we deem appropriate or in any way necessary."

Teddy, the middle-aged good ol' boy from the South, a perennial smiler with graying beard and hair, jumped between us. He sounded like the rooster in the Henery Hawk cartoon.

"Naw, naw, let's take a step back here. Nobody is trying to get anybody in trouble here. We're just here for sixteen weeks. Sister, are you saying that someone could get sent home?"

I lifted the handout, pointing to the line. "University rules are clear. Substantiated claims will result in expulsion."

Pens dropped. Angry groans could be heard from the back.

Debbie stood next to Ana. "Nobody is trying to get anybody kicked out."

Ana reached over to me and grabbed my arm. "It's getting worse."

I put my hand on hers. "I know it feels like that right now, but we can't back down on this. They have to know there are consequences."

Jack slapped his desk. "No one is going to be sent home if we have anything to do with it. We won't be hounded out like dogs. I don't care if we're in the hallowed halls of Harvard."

The men in Jack's crew and others clapped, pounded their desks, and stomped their feet in support of Jack. Jim walked in to table-thumping applause without knowing why.

After class, against the backdrop of picturesque New England, students walked in pairs by yuppie shops and restaurants: Kirk and Jack, Ana and Debbie, Liz and I.

Liz pulled at her gloves. "It's on now, mate."

I moved in closer to her to dodge the snow. "Liz, I can't believe we're going through this shit here. It's like back home, where we have to organize against assholes like this all the time. I came here to read, study, and think. I didn't come looking for any of this, but I'm not walking away."

"Yeah, mate, I'm not either. Don't get me wrong. There's a lot of queer bashing in Oz, but here, it's taken on a darker, more twisted dimension."

"I know what you mean. Everybody, even the Reasonable Guys, is open to attack. Speaking of which, there's Anthony."

Anthony crossed the street to reach us. "Either of you interested in tea? There's a great Turkish coffeehouse not far from here."

"You go ahead, mates. I've got errands," Liz said.

"I've got a little time," I said.

Anthony and I walked into a Middle Eastern coffeehouse with brass coffee urns, a grand silver tea service, and intricately woven color-patterned carpets and wall hangings. We took a window seat, the sweet aroma of Turkish tea between us.

"Thanks for what you said in class today," I said.

"Meant every word. You've got to understand, these guys get their heads in a twist over stuff like this. It's not just stuff about women. Have you heard comments about foreigners? The Japanese blokes can barely keep up."

"Look, I'm a fourth-generation Afro-Mexican Utahn. I grew up on 'go back to Mexico' rhetoric. The whole Southwest was ripped off in 1848, and most of us were already here. We didn't cross a border— the border crossed us. White people came over an ocean, so tell me, whose back is wetter?"

Anthony's beard and mustache curved up when he laughed.

"Most of our lot were criminals. Oz was settled by convicts thrust out of the British Empire. My people are Eastern European Jews, escaped the war, changed our name from Shapiro to Gleason, and settled in Oz in the forties.

BET? BET. 25

"Changed your name?" I said. "I've seen that too. I knew some Espinozas who changed their name to Thorn, but nobody was fooled. They tried so hard to pass and there was no way in hell they ever really could."

"Yeah, they make a point of finding differences when the time comes, don't they?"

"So why bother? Why bother selling off a piece of yourself like that?"

Anthony shrugged. "Look, I'm not even circumcised."

"What?"

"My parents made the decision. They're Survivors."

5 CULTURAL EXCHANGE

The student recreation room was a split-level with short steps up to a round table and chairs in the kitchen area. It adjoined a dorm room right off the kitchen. At the bottom level were a TV, a sofa, and chairs. Students met for TV, meals, and socializing. Cleo, an African American county social worker, sat with Teddy, the good-ol'-boy boilermaker from the South. Mindy, a blonde New England teachers' rep, wore an off-the-shoulder red cashmere sweater and shared photos with Sandy, a handsome, handlebar-mustached body-builder/construction worker. The Japanese students huddled around a Japanese newspaper.

Anthony and I arrived as Ana made her way up the porch steps with several pans of tinfoil-covered food. We took some of her pans. She called out as we entered the rec room.

"Will some of you guys help me get the rest of the pans from the car?" she asked.

Sandy and the Japanese students got up to help.

Jack, Kirk, Dick, and Aaron arrived. Jack kicked snow off his boots. "I hear there might be some homemade lasagna."

"There is," Ana said. "But make yourself useful and put out some plates."

"Right," Jack said. "I'll get the beer."

Ana served lasagna as she reigned over the dinner.

26

CULTURAL EXCHANGE   27

His hand over his stomach, Jack opened another beer. "This is really what I like, a good home-cooked meal." He belched.

I put my nearly full plate on the kitchen counter. "Sorry, Ana, I can hardly eat. How can you stand to feed these brutes?"

Ana turned to me with a trying-to-be-happy smile. "We've got to find a way to get along."

"I'm sorry. I can't stay," I said.

Anthony told me later what happened after I left.

Dick elbowed Jack, pointing to the Japanese students. "Now that we've had this delicious dinner, perhaps we can have some cultural exchange."

Jack took a long sip of his beer. "How about it, Kenji? How about your geisha dance?"

Kenji, clean-shaven with a slight build in his late twenties, conferred with Kenzo, a muscular man with a dark mustache. They began a stylized, synchronized dance simulating fans and exaggerated body movements. They made shrill nasal sounds and sang in a high-pitched tone, facing Jack and others, who laughed and pointed at them. Kenji and Kenzo exchanged glances as their exaggerated words and gestures mocked the watchers. The dance ended. More drinking. Most left.

Beer bottles piled up, neatly at first, then sloppily in a corner. Kenji got very drunk and could no longer stand. He sat on the couch next to Dick and tried to kiss him. Kirk took a picture. Palmer came in from the side door to find Kenji bent over the couch, his knees on the carpet.

Palmer pointed at Kenji. "What the hell is going on?! Look at him. He's sick. What are you guys doing here?"

Jack raised his beer. "What? Are you his mum?"

"I'm taking him to his room."

"You do that, mate. He needs a bit of freshening."

28 SCABMUGGERS

They laughed. Palmer pulled Kenji's arm around his neck and dragged him to the adjoining dorm room.

I'd left the rec room before the mock geisha dance and took myself to Widener Library. I stayed at the nerd citadel, with its beautiful curved ceilings, ornate clocks, crown moldings, and adornments, until closing. A stark contrast with the Robert Louis Stevenson Library in my LA hood, where I had to hide the books I wanted. I hid them because books I loved were often taken and never returned, like my favorite books in the Madeline series. I always hated closing time at the library.

I walked down the steps, my backpack heavy with books. Anthony walked down the steps from the opposite direction, and we met in the middle. He lifted his arm. "Back to the dorms? May I escort you home?"

I took his arm. "I don't see why not."

We walked together between the window-paned Harvard houses that bordered the square, over the bridge, across the Charles, home to our dorms. Snow fell like diamond dust.

✳ ✳

In class the next morning, the photo that Kirk had taken of Kenji and Dick was secretly passed around. Kenji's chair was vacant. The other Japanese students were anchored in their seats. The photo made its way to Aaron. "Looks like Dick is having a little cultural exchange," he said.

Kirk pointed to Ana. "At least he's doing better than you are."

"All in good time," Aaron said.

Aaron walked over to Ana. "Hi, Ana. How about that dinner you promised me?"

"Look, Aaron, I told you that I have a fiancé."

"It's no big deal, Ana. Just a friendly meal between classmates, that's all. Talk over assignments and readings, nothing more. How about after class today?"

CULTURAL EXCHANGE

"Okay, but not today. Maybe next week. I'll let you know."

"Just the two of us, okay, Ana? I've found a great place not too far out of town. I can get a car."

"I'll get back to you, Aaron."

Debbie unpacked her books near Ana's desk. "Why do you even talk to him?"

"Because if he thinks I'll ever go out with him, he might just leave me alone."

She was putting him off like a creditor, where all you have to do is get through right now, this moment, this call, this day. Tomorrow is tomorrow. The sad part was that she owed him nothing more than a solid no.

Back at his seat, Aaron flashed a thumbs-up sign to Kirk.

We settled in for the morning. The nerd contingent tested their pens and pulled out clean sheets of paper. Some of us dated the page. Howard Zinn was the day's lecturer. In a brief exchange before I entered class, Elise had introduced me to him. I told him I had all the course books but his was the only one I'd already read cover to cover.

Jack muttered, "What have we got today—Elise's latest communist?"

Palmer turned to Jack. "I heard that. Even you can't argue with Howard Zinn's work, Jack. He's one of the most read labor historians in the country, if not the entire industrialized West."

"Yeah, we get that commie pap at home as well. I've even read some of it."

Palmer leaned into the back of his chair close to Jack. "We just might be able to win you over."

Denny overheard Palmer and Jack. "Indeed, we might have to call you Comrade Jack."

The class blew up in laughter.

Jack winced. "I will not accept any such appellation."

Liz turned to Jack. "Oh, but mate, it suits you so."

More laughter.

Kirk turned to Jack. "Oh, c'mon, Jack, be a sport."

The class was bent over with laughter. The red on Jack's face reached his ears, neck, arms, and clenched fists.

Elise and Zinn walked in. Kenji had been waiting by the door. He approached Elise and whispered something to her. She nodded, and then she and Zinn left. Kenji stood in front of the class, his head down, with a piece of paper in his hands. He stood until the class got quiet; then he began to read.

"I wish to offer my sincere apology for my recent actions. I've brought dishonor to my colleagues, my classmates, and to myself. I pledge to conduct myself in a respectful manner from here forward. Thank you."

Kenji folded himself into a deep bow and took his seat.

Whispers back and forth. The other Japanese students stared straight ahead. Palmer's seat was next to Kenji's and a row down from my seat. Palmer put his hand on Kenji's back. "I know that was hard. I'll see you at the dorm later." Kenji gathered his things and left.

Declan O'Hara wrote something on his desk name card.

Palmer turned to Jack. "Are you happy now, assholes?"

Elise and Zinn returned. Zinn opened his notes at the lectern. "What is working-class history? It's the history of the men and women who went to war, who died, who survived and came back to work in the factories and fields. Did they work for themselves? No. They worked for others. Who did they die for? Not for their communities, as they were led to believe. They died for the interests of those who bought and sold their labor at the lowest price possible. What is the history that we are taught? We are taught the history of those who bought and sold the labor of working people, not the history of the workers themselves. So, why is working people's history important? It's important because it's the history of women and men

CULTURAL EXCHANGE

who actually work, who make things, who power an economy, whose labor powers the world."

No one spoke. Everything we had been taught about history had been turned on its head in a single, brief monologue. The battles of the rich for the spoils of war were what we had been taught—not the valiant, heroic sacrifices of everyday people who dared to rise up and demand fair pay for their labor. Their history was never told.

 **MILL GIRLS**

One morning, we boarded a bus to the Mill Museum in Lowell, Massachusetts. Cleo and Teddy sat together. Debbie and Ana sat together opposite the aisle from Aaron, who sat as close to Ana as he could get. I sat with Anthony. There was something comfortably familiar about him, our shared insider/outsider experience in the WASP worlds we lived in. An unspoken understanding that we could never really let our guard down, except with each other. My then Jewish husband back home always admonished me to keep my papers in order, my money in cash, and a smile on my face. Anthony understood that. I didn't know then that I had Jewish ancestors, but I felt the closeness, a kinship, almost, between us. We were also both in long-term marriages, with children, and filled a role of companionship for each other.

As the bus turned onto the highway, Ana stood and lifted her arms like a conductor. "Who's got a song?"

"How about 'The Internationale'?" I said. "All verses?"

Liz reached over to Jack. "Perhaps our comrade would like to lead us."

Palmer joined in with Claude and Denny. "Yeah, Comrade Jack, how about it?"

Jack sat red-faced between Kirk and Dick in the back-window seat. They pointed at Jack, bent over in laughter, nearly out of breath. Jack's blue eyes bulged as he fumed.

MILL GIRLS

At the museum, we squeezed into the dining room of a turn-of-the-twentieth-century historic New England clapboard house around a cramped, spartan dinner table with facsimile food on it. Life-size wall posters showed mill girls in period clothing as they stood by mill machines. The images progressed to posters showing mill girls at rallies and on strike. They were Irish, Italian, Eastern European, and other nationalities.

Her hair pulled back in a silver bun, the docent wore a business suit and crepe-soled shoes. She pointed to the table.

"What you see here is a typical mill girl meal: bread, bacon, and some meat. The girls were sent to these dormitories by their families. They worked long hours—often twelve, sometimes fourteen hours a day. It was important to their families that some semblance of respectability be preserved, so the girls were housed here under the watchful eye of the house matron. The house matron was employed by the mill. She ran the dormitory and maintained a strict curfew. She also handled delicate matters such as monitoring the girls' menstrual cycles, and, if necessary, discreetly sent them home."

Liz and I blurted out the same question. "Were any of the men sent home?"

Jack jumped in before the docent could respond. "Seems like the mill was an equal opportunity employer, wouldn't you say, mates? Genuinely concerned with preserving the respectability and reputation of the fine young ladies housed here."

Liz turned to Jack. "There's nothing respectable about hard, dirty work twelve hours a day under a foreman and under the watch of a matron at night. And who knows what else their bosses subjected them to?"

The docent opened a curtain to show the house next door. "The men's dorms were run differently. They lived communally, mainly for economic reasons, although the mill ran both dormitories for a profit. Men paid a portion of their pay to the mill for their berths.

Mill girls were paid less than the men, so a larger portion of their pay went for mill housing."

Liz turned to me. "Forced to work long hours and live in cramped quarters, required to pay more, and imprisoned by matrons? No wonder they rebelled."

"Aye, Comrade Jack," I said. "Maybe Marx was right. Capitalism sows the seeds of its own destruction."

Denny looked up from the historical notes at the end of the mill girls' dinner table. "Indeed, a classic case of working-class concentration of labor, agitation, and subsequent rebellion."

The women and some of the men laughed. Jack's face flushed a new shade of red, and he spoke almost inaudibly. "Just what I need—a snowflake quoting that Jew to me."

Denny stepped closer to Jack. "What was that, Jack? I couldn't quite hear you."

Kirk and Dick moved in behind Jack. Jack turned to Denny. "Haven't you read *Animal Farm*, Denny? Isn't there a character called Snowflake? I'm sorry if I'm mistaken."

Denny left. Jack swelled a wide grin and walked away with Kirk and Dick in tow. *Typical chickenshit racist—never able to come right out with it*, I thought.

✳ ✳

Liz and I were washing our hands in the museum lavatory. Debbie was in a stall. I pulled down a paper towel to wipe my hands. "Poor Denny, and did you hear what Jack said about Jews?"

Liz pulled a paper towel. "Yes, did you see Denny's face? This has gone too far."

I wiped the sink. "Liz, he's hit just about everybody. I wonder if Anthony heard it?"

Liz wadded up her towel. "How could he miss it? It's not just him. I got a raft from Declan the other day about my kind being an abomination."

MILL GIRLS 35

Debbie called out from the stall. "That fits. Just look at Declan's desk name card. He's got a week-to-week chronology with racist, sexist, and bigoted epithets on it summarizing each week. The first week it said 'Amazon's Revenge.'"

"He has what?" I asked, throwing away my wadded-up paper towel.

Just then, Ana came in. She shut the restroom door behind her and stood with her back to it, her hands and arms spread out like Spiderman scaling a wall. We turned to her. "What? What happened to you? Did something happen?"

Debbie came out of the stall. "It's Aaron again, isn't it?"

Ana looked away, started to say something, and left. We all locked eyes.

"It's got to stop," Liz said. "We've got to tell Elise it's Aaron."

Debbie washed her hands. "It won't do any good. I already told her I would. Ana will deny it. He seems to leave her alone when other people are around."

"That's it," I said. "We'll organize shifts to walk her to and from class every day."

Debbie pulled a paper towel. "She goes home on the weekends, so we just have to cover the weekdays. Who are we down to now? Just the four of us?"

Liz checked her hair in the mirror. "Cleo's gone off with Teddy, and Mindy's been AWOL with Sandy for days."

I grabbed my backpack. "That's it, then—the four of us. I'm sure some of the Reasonable Guys will help."

"Look, mates, I'm glad we've got a plan for Ana. Count me in. But I'm being openly dyke-baited."

I pulled on my backpack. "You're right, Liz. We've got to do more than just react."

✳ ✳

It turned out that Ana had gotten away from the group and found herself alone in the mill girls' sleeping quarters. She described the scene to me later: There were rows of bunk beds stacked three high, thin mattresses on wood slats. Dresses, petticoats, shirtwaists, and aprons hung on wall hooks; a washbasin and water pitcher sat on a table at the end of each row of beds. A tall mirror hung over each washbasin. Wall-size posters showed mill girls at meals and in group photos. She told me how she had touched their beds, the washbasin, the hanging aprons and clothes.

Ana said, "I saw my own face in the faces of the mill girls in the pictures. I straightened my back and walked taller. That's when I saw Aaron in the mirror. He opened the door. I slammed it shut, locked it, and left through another door. I got away."

"Is that when you came into the bathroom at the museum and we were all there?" I asked.

"Yes, but I didn't tell you then because everyone was there. It was just too much."

"It's okay. We have a plan."

7 THIS IS OUR SHOT

We huddled under coats for the morning's lecture like it would make a difference to the new nor'easter headed our way.

At the lectern, Izzy Mac, a balding man in his mid-fifties wearing glasses, a bow tie, and a functional suit, put down his briefcase. "Elise has asked me to teach this section on arbitration. The best way to learn how to do an arbitration is to do one. Some of you have experience and others don't, so I'm going to mix you up a bit. Now listen to these facts as I assign you your roles. Simone, you are going to represent a member who has been fired for allegedly harassing a coworker. Jack, you'll represent the coworker who has complained and was removed from her workplace. She wants to go back and believes she is being retaliated against for complaining."

I sank a stare into Izzy. "Is this a setup? Everybody knows what's going on here."

Izzy leaned one elbow on top of the lectern toward me. "No. No setup. This outline was prepared well before you got here. It's a typical case, one I'm sure you've encountered before."

Jack balled his fists. "What if they don't want her back?"

Both elbows on his books, Izzy nodded. "Good prep questions. Remember, Jack, you're her advocate. Have your case outline and witness list to me by tomorrow."

I gaped at Izzy again. "Tomorrow!"

"Yes, tomorrow. You should be able to digest the case well enough

37

to establish your theory and make up a witness list. Simone, as you're leading the case for the union, you'll assemble the union's team. Simone and Jack, you are on the same side. Different interests, but on the same side."

Jack threw his books into his backpack. "I don't know anything about American rules on this."

Izzy leaned back. "Just try it like you would back home, Jack. By now you must know that having the fight is more important than knowing the rules."

Jack slung his backpack over his shoulder. "Who's the arbitrator?"

"I am, of course. Anyone want to be management?"

The entire class shot daggers at Izzy.

Debbie and I welcomed Palmer, Anthony, Liz, Ana, and Denny to our dorm after class. Amid stacks of papers on the coffee table, Ana piled up discarded take-out boxes. I put up butcher paper. "Where's Jack? We've got to get ready."

Ana collected empty cans. "Not coming. I told him it was about arb prep."

I pulled out a marker. "Just as well. This is our chance to tell our story."

Palmer took out his notepad. "I think we'd better do this straight and not use the arbitration training to further divide the class."

I uncapped the marker. "It's already divided. Too late to play by the rules. Besides, that's not why we're here."

"But aren't we supposed to get technical training too?"

"Don't you get it? We're not supposed to be technicians. We're supposed to lead."

Liz pulled out her notebook. "Simone's right. We've got to get this story out. Ana, you've got to be our star witness."

Denny scanned the documents in front of him. "I must say, what I know about your legal system here, there is little room for the truth. We must break it out. We must liberate it."

THIS IS OUR SHOT

I faced the blank page. "We've got this one shot."

Anthony shifted his seat next to Ana. "We've got to take it. What do you say, Ana?"

Ana clutched her hands. "Okay, okay. What do I do?"

I pushed aside the stacked documents in front of Ana. "Ana, all you have to do is tell your story. Talk about what's actually been happening to you since you got here. I'll ask you basic introductory questions, but it's your story to tell."

She clenched her hands more tightly. "No more class disruption, please."

I put down the marker. "The class is already disrupted. We've all been carrying the weight of it for too long, especially you. It's time to get this story out. Elise won't be able to contain it if we involve the other faculty. And Jack and the assholes just might tip their hands. This is our shot."

Ana buried her clenched hands in her lap. "But what about the actual mock arbitration case?"

I flipped back the blank butcher sheet. "I've already outlined it. I'll argue for a dismissal. It's the boss's burden to prove their case against our grievant by a preponderance of the evidence. That's a fifty-per-cent-plus-one standard. They can't get in the door with this record, no primary evidence, no admission, no secondary evidence or even circumstantial evidence. All they've got is an unsigned statement. Our guy denies anything happened. Her word against his. She didn't even sign the statement. She's not willing to go on the record and thinks management went too far by firing the guy, so they can't rely on her testimony even if they try to compel it. Based on this record, our guy walks."

Ana pressed her open hands in her thighs. "But won't they be upset if we hijack their arbitration?"

"They'll be alarmed that the story's out more than they'll care about a paper case. What are they going to do—retaliate against us for exposing an abuser? Doing it this way buys everyone cover, and we'll have turned the tables on them. And you won't be alone—we'll all be right there with you."

Two days later, at the hearing, the classroom was arranged in a trial setting: the union team on one side, management on the other behind a stack of books and documents three feet high to hide whoever was there. Izzy, the arbitrator, sat in the middle. "Are we ready to proceed?"

I read the list on my legal pad. "Yes, Mr. Arbitrator. To begin, we have a new witness."

Jack pushed back in his chair. "Hold on. What's Ana doing here?"

"Our witness has been in hiding, Mr. Arbitrator."

"Hiding from who? I object!"

Izzy looked at both of us. "It's unusual to have objections from the same side of the table."

Izzy turned to me. "This is highly irregular, Ms. Arroyo." Then to Jack: "Mr. Wright, you are representing the member alleging the harassment who wants to go back to her old workplace. This part of the case is not your member's issue. Ms. Arroyo, is this witness's testimony germane?"

"Mr. Arbitrator, with respect to issues of sexual harassment and abuse, yes, I believe it is."

"I'll allow it, then, and weigh the merits during my deliberations."

"Thank you, Mr. Arbitrator, but before I introduce the witness, I argue for the dismissal of employer's case."

"On what basis?"

"The employer hasn't met its burden of proof."

"Go on."

"To establish just cause to discipline my member, the employer must meet the standard of proof by a preponderance of the evidence.

THIS IS OUR SHOT

Based on these facts, the disciplinary action against my member can't be sustained. Therefore, I argue for dismissal."

"Please elaborate."

"Management's case rests on the accuser's unsigned statement. Even if the statement were to be admitted, the grievant would be denied the right to question his accuser because his accuser refused to formalize the claim. Therefore, there is no evidence against him."

"Is there a response from the employer?"

Papers flew up from behind a tower of books and files on the management side. Izzy waited. "Hearing no response, the employer can address your arguments in their opening."

"Thank you, Mr. Arbitrator," I said.

"Let's proceed."

"I call Ana Maria Spretto."

Jack jumped to his feet. "Ana? What's Ana got to do with this? I object."

Izzy gaveled. "I already ruled that her testimony would be admitted, Mr. Wright. Please sit down. Ms. Spretto, please raise your right hand. Do you affirm that the evidence you are about to give is truthful and accurate?"

"I do."

Kirk walked in late, obviously hungover. "What the hell is going on here? Why is Ana there?"

He reached over to Jack. "Call a recess."

Jack raised his hand. "Your honor, I mean Mr. Arbitrator. I want a recess."

Izzy gaveled. "Request denied. Mr. Wright, your case starts when this one ends. Ms. Arroyo, this better be on track."

"Thank you, Mr. Arbitrator."

Ana leaned over to me. "I don't think I can do this."

"Ana, this is our shot. We're all behind you."

Liz, Denny, Anthony, Palmer, Debbie, Claude, and others sat behind Ana. Aaron, Dick, and Kirk sat opposite her.

42 SCABMUGGERS

"I'm sorry. I can't," she whispered.

"Ana, look at me. It's okay."

"No, really, I'm not feeling well."

I tried to hide my disappointment by taking a breath and staring at the notes on the page in front of me. We were *this* close, but she wasn't ready.

I took her arm. "Are you sure?"

"Really, I'm not well."

"Okay. I'll let him know."

Izzy turned to the union side of the table. "Ms. Arroyo, Mr. Wright, please approach."

When we reached the bench, Izzy asked, "Ms. Arroyo, are you prepared to proceed?"

"I ask that Ana be excused."

Jack pushed his face into mine. "She shouldn't have been here in the first damn place."

I pushed mine into his. "You won't get away with this."

"Get away with what? I won't be harassed by you."

"You're the harasser here!"

Jack turned to Izzy. "I want an investigation into these allegations." *How rich—the harasser who claims harassment.*

"Yes," I said. "Let's have an investigation. Let's have a full investigation."

Izzy motioned for us both to sit down. "Sit down, you two. Nobody is going to investigate anybody."

✳ ✳

The next morning, his elbows on his notes, Izzy addressed the class. "I'm ready to render my decision. Notwithstanding the irregular approach to this case, it is my ruling that the employer failed to meet its burden of proof by a preponderance of the evidence. Based on this record, the disciplinary action against the grievant cannot be

THIS IS OUR SHOT

sustained. This does not mean that what is alleged didn't happen. It simply means that there can be no finding that it did. The grievant goes back to work. He's entitled to full back pay. He is to be made whole in every way with no record of this in his personnel file. So ordered." Izzy pounded the gavel.

Jack stood. "What about my member?"

"She stays where she is."

"That doesn't seem fair. Why not move him instead of her?"

"Nothing was proven against him."

"But she didn't do anything."

"She got what she wanted. She raised an issue and got the harassment stopped. Look at it this way: Ms. Arroyo loses by winning. An alleged offender goes back to work, perhaps, one hopes, if the allegations are true, chastened but nonetheless free from discipline in this instance. And you win by losing. Your grievant stopped short of naming her harasser and stops the harassment but pays a price for her silence. So ordered."

* *

After class, Anthony and I went for Turkish coffee. As Anthony stirred his demitasse, he said, "You did a great job on the mock arbitration case in class today, even though the Ana case fell through. You should have seen them, Kirk, Dick, and the others, when you won. They were cheering you on, but it was you, so they had to hold back. It was hilarious."

"Score a victory for Jack."

"It's not a defeat to regroup to fight another day."

"Depends on what you've given up to win and what there's left to fight with. Winning for assholes isn't why I'm in this."

"What do you mean? There's more to this, isn't there?"

"Yeah, for example, in the thirties the Wagner Act was created to guarantee the right to collective bargaining, yet it excluded agricultural and domestic workers, mostly Black workers, in a concession to the racist South." I moved my cup closer to me as if to protect it.

"In the forties the Taft-Hartley Act nearly gutted the Wagner Act, outlawing closed shops and the secondary boycott, for example."

Anthony looked up from his cup. "Did that mean you couldn't make everyone pay dues and strike to support another union?"

Both hands on my cup, I said, "Yes."

"And in the fifties, unions who wouldn't sign noncommunist loyalty oaths during the Red Scare were attacked."

I took a last sip of my tea. "The worst of it was that local union halls were raided by anti-communist mobs, union members. Their members were beaten, maimed, and jailed by other union members."

Anthony looked up from his cup. "The right wing must've been terrified."

I covered my empty teacup with a napkin. "To cap it all off, in the fifties the AFL-CIO leadership under George Meany cut a deal with capital that all but wiped out the movement. During the Red Scare, the AFL-CIO turned on their own members at the behest of the boss."

I pushed my cup away. "Historically, when faced with a threat to themselves, they committed fratricide, first against the Wobblies in the twenties, then against the communists in the fifties, the only two unions who were organizing and integrating unions. Racist from the start."

Anthony looked in his empty cup. "What did you expect them to do? Risk what little they'd gained for some ideal?"

"What little they gained wasn't worth saving at the expense of the people whose blood and sweat won it for them."

"Oh, come on. My people have been sold out for centuries."

"Maybe that's the difference between us. I expect them to live up to what they say they stand for."

"I have no reason to have that expectation."

"I can't afford not to have it," I said.

THIS IS OUR SHOT

"But as you said, they raided and attacked their own members."

"That's true, but soon enough, there'll be more of us than there are of them."

"So, you're waiting to return the favor?"

"No, they're still our class brothers and sisters. We need each other, even if they don't know it. Anybody who's been stomped on and has any humanity left can't do that to someone else. Nelson was right, in South Africa white people's fear was more dangerous than Black people's rage."

Anthony pushed his empty cup away next to mine. "Maybe it's the reason I'm attracted to you. You believe in this movement's ideals, even in the face of its barbarity."

"I'm no Pollyanna. It's simple, our history shows they can't make it without us and we can't make it without them. If the bosses can buy us off to kill one another, no one wins."

Anthony took my hand, pulled me close, and tried to kiss me. I pulled my hand back and turned away.

"No, Anthony, I have a husband, children. I'm not free to pursue that kind of relationship with you."

"I know. I know. I have a family too."

I reached to take his hand. "But we can be friends, can't we?"

He took my hand. "Yes," he said. "We can."

Here it was again, blurred lines in combat. A campaign high that merges everything. I'd been through this before, but win, lose, or draw, when the campaign's over, if you acted on the impulses, inevitably you looked at the other person and wondered what you were thinking. I didn't want that for either of us.

CLASS SPEAKER

The next morning, the class had settled in. Elise was at the podium. "Now, listen up. I am going to announce the rules for selecting this year's class speaker. Labor secretary William Gould will be the keynote speaker at commencement. One or perhaps two of you will be selected by your peers to make an address on behalf of the class. What you say will matter. We strongly urge a balance that reflects the diverse representation of this class, by race, gender, public/private sector, and national/international. You get two votes each. The election will be held a week from today. Any questions?"

I raised my hand. "Do we have to select two candidates?"

"Not necessarily."

Palmer reached over to me. "What are you thinking?"

Jack stood. "Are we required to adhere to your parameters?"

Elise leaned forward on the lectern toward Jack. "All you have ever been asked to do, Jack, is to bring your talented brain to this class. So, no, although you don't have to adhere to the suggested parameters, they are strongly recommended."

Claude turned to face Jack. "Yes, Comrade Jack, your uniquely talented brain is all that is required."

The class laughed. Jack spat out his words. "I said I did not wish to be called that!"

After class we broke up into groups and huddled in the back of

CLASS SPEAKER

the room. Liz came over. "Mate, what were you working out in class with Elise?"

"Let's get our lists out. Liz, if we pick one person, we can double our votes."

"So, you mean bullet our votes, mate?"

"Yes, that way we can focus on one candidate and select a woman class speaker."

"Right! I bet she'll have a lot to say about the plight of women in the workplace and what's been going on here."

"I bet she would."

Palmer joined in. "You mean not split our votes?"

"Yes, use both our votes for one candidate."

Palmer pulled out his tattered list. "What's the count?"

I matched my list to his. "We've been able to tally at least fifteen of us for our Ana campaign, six women and nine men."

Palmer went through the lists. "If we get two votes each, that's thirty out of sixty possible votes. We could get a majority for one candidate."

"Exactly."

"Let's get to work, mates."

Late one Sunday, Debbie and I left our dorm door slightly open to wait for Ana. Liz and Anthony were there. Ana came in with foil-covered food pans and knocked.

I opened the door. "Hi, Ana, we were hoping you'd come."

"I brought some cannoli from home."

Liz got up to help Ana with one of the trays. "Did you make it, Ana?"

I grabbed a tray. "Come in. Let me get that."

Ana took off her coat. "What's been happening here? I didn't have time to make the shells, but I made the filling. What are you guys doing here?"

Liz put the tray down. "Sit. It's not good news, I'm afraid, mate."

48   SCABMUGGERS

"Why? What happened?"

Debbie moved a pillow to make room for Ana. "It seems that Palmer and some of the Reasonable Guys went to a strip club with Jack and company on Friday."

I took Ana's coat and purse. "And they had a meeting on Saturday, to which none of the women were invited, where they decided that they would vote to have no class speaker."

"They did what?!"

"Yeah, mate, the men met and decided there would be no class speaker."

"I can't believe this. Palmer too?"

Anthony made more room for Ana on the sofa. Anthony was part of our crew; we all needed him and his support. As his comrade in arms, so to speak, I relied on him to respect the boundary I'd set and didn't want anything he felt for me to affect our collective work together. Most importantly, I hoped I could count on his friendship, which I valued.

"No," Anthony said. "They didn't want him or me at the Saturday meeting and only told him about it the next day. That's how I found out. I didn't get asked either."

Ana got up from the couch. "I'm going to call Declan myself. None of you were invited?"

I handed her the phone. "Here, call him from here."

Ana dialed. "Hi, Declan, I just got back from Rhode Island and heard about a meeting that happened this weekend. I want to talk to you about it. Okay. Okay. I'll meet you in the rec room. Ten minutes. Fine."

Ana gathered her coat and purse. "I'll see you guys later."

Anthony had gone by the time Ana got back from her meeting with Declan. Ana took off her coat and sat on the sofa. Debbie was on the edge of her seat. "What happened?"

"When I got to the rec room, Declan was already there, so I just came out with it: 'So, what's this I hear about a meeting over the weekend?'

"'Yeah,' he said, 'some of us guys got together to see what we could do about our problems in class.'

"I looked right at him," Ana said. "'*Us guys?*'

"Then he tried to give me this line about if I had been in town, I would've been invited. But I wasn't buying it. I told him you guys were here and if he was all that concerned about class unity, he could have invited you or waited till I got home and invited all of us."

When Ana asked him about Liz and me, he said the guys thought that meeting among themselves first made the most sense.

"I couldn't believe what he was saying," Ana told us. "I said to him, 'So, you made decisions about us and didn't include us?' He said he knew it sounded like that, but it wasn't. I was starting to get pissed off, so I said, 'It sure sounds like it was like that.'

"'Believe me, Ana,' he said, 'it really wasn't. In the interest of class unity, we decided to have no class speaker.'

"'What?!' I said. 'You *decided*!' I mean, I couldn't believe it."

When Ana pressed him, he kept on and said, "Given the problems we've been having, it made sense not to divide the class further by running an election."

"I looked right at him and told him to his face, 'You know we're planning to run a candidate.'

"'Yes,' he said. 'And, like I said, in the interest of class unity, we decided not to support any candidate.'

"You know what, Declan?" Ana said. "I'm finally starting to understand."

"I knew you would, Ana."

"Yeah, Declan," she said. "It's all making a lot more sense to me now."

There on the couch with us, as she told us what happened, Ana folded her arms close against her body like she did when she held her muff tight in a storm. "I got up, and he helped me with my coat. 'Really, Ana,' he said. 'No one is trying to leave anyone out. I know the guys would have invited you if you had been here. I'm sure of it.'

"I left and came back here. I can't believe they'd go that far. And I can't believe Declan would try to bullshit me like that. Does he think I'm stupid? Do they all think that?"

I shifted closer to Ana. "Nobody thinks you're stupid."

"So, as I was leaving," she said, "I told him that none of them would get any cannoli."

Liz got her coat. "Oh, I bet that stopped 'im, mate."

I turned away to hide a laugh. "Yeah, that must have hurt 'im real bad."

Debbie faced Liz and me. "Stop it, you guys."

"Okay, okay, I'm sorry, Ana," I said. "Let's get ready for this vote."

Liz pulled on a glove. "It's going to be close."

Ana got up to put her coat on. "Where's Mindy? Where's Cleo?"

"We appear to have lost them, mate," Liz said, pulling on her other glove.

Ana took a cannoli tray. "What happened to them?"

I looked over at Debbie. "Tell her."

"Tell me what?" Ana asked, balancing the cannoli.

I lowered my eyes. "She has to know."

Debbie pulled her hair back. "Well, okay. The other day, I walked into the rec room after the guys had their meeting. I didn't know they were having one. Anyway, I walked in because I was supposed to meet Palmer there. That's when I saw Mindy. First, she was dancing with Declan upstairs in the kitchen. Several of the guys were standing around with beers. Mindy started to kiss Kirk, then Dick. She was being passed around. There must have been ten guys there. I kept looking without them seeing me, but I couldn't see Palmer. Finally, Sandy picked Mindy up and took her to his room, carrying her over his shoulder. The others laughed and called her horrible names. They didn't see me because I didn't go upstairs. I was about to leave when I heard Palmer's voice. He'd just come in from the upstairs side door connecting his room to the rec room. Palmer didn't see me at first either. He called to them, 'Will you guys keep it down in here?'

"Kirk raised his beer. 'Sandy just got the goods, Palmer. A bunch of us are going into town to see what we can find, or are you being taken care of by your resident geisha, Kenji?'

"'Fuck yourself. Have you guys seen Debbie? I was supposed to meet her here.'

"Jack elbowed Kirk. 'Debbie? Not bad, ey, blokes?'

"Palmer said, 'Fuck you, Jack,' and shut the door.

"I went next door to Palmer's. That's what happened."

Ana wrung her hands. "Did they see you?"

"I don't think so. Has anyone seen Mindy since then?"

Liz shook her head. "She hasn't slept in her room for two nights. Cleo spends all her time with Teddy. We hardly see them."

Ana unclenched her hands and pushed her palms into her thighs. "Looks like it's down to the four of us."

There are always defections in campaigns. You can count on it. As this was Ana's first time in this kind of battle, it was hard to share this inevitable loss with her. Still, she didn't flinch.

THE GREAT CANNOLI LOCKOUT

The next morning, the class gathered in small groups, Jack, Kirk, Dickand Declan at one end of the room, the Japanese students at another. Sitting near the cannoli, Anthony took slow and sensuous bites of cannoli, smacked his lips, wiped his mouth, put away a third, and patted his stomach. "Nothing quite like this in Aussie."

Jack and company watched. Rick walked over to Ana. "Is it true, Ana? We can't have any cannoli?"

"You heard."

"God, what'd we do?"

"You guys know what you did."

Eddie, a Midwestern steelworker who usually sat away from Jack and company, came over to talk to Ana. "Hi, Ana, aren't you taking this a little too seriously? I mean, no cannoli, that's a bit too far, don't you think?"

"You made your choice when you went to that meeting."

Liz and I sat and watched The Great Cannoli Lockout as Ana turned away anyone who had been at the meeting. We looked over at Jack and company. I elbowed Liz. "I can't believe it. Look at them."

"Yeah, mate, she's hit them harder than any feminist diatribe we could come up with."

We laughed as Palmer approached. "Is it true, mate, that you were out with the rogues?"

"Don't give me grief," he said. "I went when I got wind that something was up to see if I could work something out."

Liz shook her head. "Well, what happened?"

"You know what happened. Does that mean I don't get any cannoli?"

"I don't know, mate. That's up to Ana. You'd better hurry, though. The cannoli are starting to lose their shape, actually, have become rather soft and drippy. You know, like a limp dick. Not that I would know anything about that."

Liz and I laughed and high-fived each other.

We had history with Jim Green the next morning. "Okay, listen up," he said. "We've got lots of stuff to cover today. Some of you will give your presentations, and we'll finish the footage on Aliquippa today."

Jim turned the lights off. On the screen there was footage of the shootings at Aliquippa, Pennsylvania. People were fleeing. Police were shooting them down. The chairman of Little Steel explained that they had no choice. Bodies were lying around on the ground. The video stopped, and Jim shifted his notes. "What happened at Aliquippa?"

Several hands went up, including Ana's, Liz's, Debbie's, and mine. Jim pointed to Debbie. "It was a classic company town. The company owned everything. The United Steelworkers came in and organized. People gathered for a picnic, company goons opened fire, killing people, shooting some in the back."

"Who was held responsible?"

The same hands went up. Jim pointed to me. "The Left got the blame in the press."

Palmer answered without raising his hand. "But suppressed, later-released footage showed that the people were unarmed. The company police did the shooting."

"Who won?"

Jack answered without raising his hand. "Little Steel won that one."

"What was significant about it for the Steelworkers? Hands, please."

The same hands went up. Jim pointed to Liz. Frustrated, Ana put her hand down. "Even though Little Steel won, the Steelworkers didn't lose."

"How so?"

Once again, the same hands went up. Jim pointed to me.

"There was a public outcry about the massacre, and even though the Steelworkers almost got wiped out, they managed to build an organization inside the town and all but dismantle the company store system."

"Right. So even though the Steelworkers lost the subsequent election, they won a fundamental change in the company town system, forever changing the way steel companies ran the lives of American workers. So, Liz is right, even if you lose you can still win."

✳ ✳

Izzy walked into the classroom after lunch, loaded down with newspapers. "Glad you're all here. The paper this morning has a story about union density, and I have copies for you."

As Izzy passed out the copies of the article, Anthony walked in wearing a sweatshirt with "Harvard" written in Hebrew on the back of it and sat down next to Jack. Izzy handed a copy of the article to Anthony. "Impressive," Izzy said.

I sat opposite Anthony and smiled.

Izzy walked back to the lectern. "Since we had so much fun with the last arbitration I thought we might try it again. Who read the case?"

The class groaned.

Jack looked over at Kenji. "I'll bet Kenji would love to explain the legal theory for us, wouldn't you, Kenji?"

THE GREAT CANNOLI LOCKOUT

55

Kenji fumbled for his translation device. Palmer looked back at Jack. "Maybe you would, Jack?"

"Maybe I would, but maybe I'd like to hear another international perspective. How about it, Kenji?"

Izzy dropped a book on the lectern. "It's so exciting to see such enthusiastic participation. Jack, you'll get your turn. I'll let you know. Who can tell me what's going on in this case?"

Ana, Aaron, and I raised our hands.

Izzy pointed to Aaron. "The Brotherhood of Locomotive Firemen and Enginemen refused to represent a Black member who had been fired. The NAACP's then lead counsel, Thurgood Marshall, sued. The railway union lost."

"Well done. Succinct. So, what do you make of this? What was going on here? Was this typical of union practices? Or was this an unusual case?"

Ana's hand was up. Anthony spoke without raising his hand.

"Unfortunately, it was all too common."

Cleo rose up from her notes. "This was the fifties. Jim Crow was alive and kicking."

Ana's hand was still up.

Izzy looked past her. "In unions?"

Palmer spoke without raising his hand. "Of course, in unions. The AFL-CIO refused to acknowledge the leadership of A. Philip Randolph, president of the Sleeping Car Porters, or count his members as full members until he broke away to form his own organization."

Tired of having her hand up, Ana put her hand down.

Izzy stepped around the lectern. "I thought unions were supposed to defend the rights of its own members."

I spoke without raising my hand. "Not all of its union members. It wasn't unusual for there to be dual seniority lists, one for Blacks, one for whites. Lower pay for Blacks and women workers and Jim Crow union halls."

Jack slammed his notebook shut. "Now you're going to tell me the commies set us free."

Liz turned to Jack. "Since you asked, Comrade Jack, it's apparent that communists were developing Black and Latino leadership in the unions they led."

Izzy shifted back to his notes at the lectern. "You're going to have to save the political analysis for another class. I want to bring you back to these facts."

Aaron stood. "Izzy, before we move on, I'd just like to say that I think it was because of what was going on that A. Philip Randolph was forced to rely on the socialists."

I stood. "C'mon, you've got that all backward. A. Philip Randolph was a socialist who himself organized and led the Sleeping Car Porters and eventually the rest of the labor movement."

Izzy looked at his watch. "Any last comments before we get back to the law?"

Palmer stood. "It was his idea to start the March on Washington."

I faced Aaron. "It's a disservice to his memory and to what he stood for to say that he was anyone's dupe, much less a socialist dupe."

"Any more comments?" Izzy asked, looking back at his watch.

Jack stood up. "Look, it's well known that the Bolshies took their cues from Moscow. They weren't interested in building the labor movement, only in building their own power base. And I say they got what they deserved."

I slapped my pen down. "Got what they *deserved*? Beaten, maimed, imprisoned, raided by their own unions!"

"You've got to do what you've got to do to defend democracy, ey, blokes?"

"Defend democracy?!" I repeated. "How is it a defense of democracy to maim and kill dissent?"

Palmer stood. "Yeah, look what we're left with. Less than ten percent organized, all in the name of democracy. Right!"

THE GREAT CANNOLI LOCKOUT   57

Denny stood to face everyone. "Looks like the US labor movement shot its own members in the back. Aliquippa turned inward."

Jack whispered to Kirk, "Save me from the Zulu warrior."

✳ ✳

After class, Liz and I had dinner at the dorm dining hall. Palmer put his plate down and joined us. "I've just done a new vote count. We're almost there. The Japanese students aren't saying how they'll vote."

Liz put her fork down. "Jack's been stepping up his anti-Asian campaign."

I unfolded my napkin. "Makes sense, he would do that now."

"Yeah, mate. He banks on fear. It's his only currency. He knows they will vote based on perceived retribution."

Palmer buttered a roll. "Right. I've talked to Kenji about what this vote means, but there is no way to guarantee the harassment will stop after the vote."

I picked up my fork. "But there is no way to guarantee that it will end if they vote with him either."

Palmer cut into his roll. "But Jack can guarantee that it will get worse."

"That's it, mate."

I stabbed some lettuce. "But can't they see that if we stick together it's the only chance we've got to stop the harassment for all of us?"

Palmer buttered his roll. "All they know is that some of them have been turned into geishas. They don't understand what's going on in class most of the time, and they really don't feel like part of the class."

"Right, mate, they're only looking at lessening the pain. They've accepted that pain is a given."

I stabbed more lettuce.

"Palmer, how can we reach them?"

"I do have to say, mate, there are no Japanese women here."

58   SCABMUGGERS

"Yeah, that's true," I said, "and they treat us like we don't exist half the time either."

Palmer cut into another roll. "I'm not so sure it's about you personally or the women in the class. It's what they're getting from the guys."

"You do have to admit, mate, they don't have a very female-friendly culture."

Palmer took a bite of his roll and nodded. "It's true."

I pushed my plate aside and took a look at the list. "We've got to do something. Let's recheck the numbers. I'm not sure we've got everybody we think we have."

Declan came into the dining room and walked over to our table. "Simone, can I talk to you for a minute?"

I looked to Palmer and Liz.

"It'll only take a minute," he said.

Palmer and Liz nodded.

Declan opened the door to the patio. "I'll get to the point. Who are you running?"

"We're backing Liz."

"Have you considered a slate?"

"No, we're concentrating on one candidate. We suspect you are too."

"We're not as organized as you are."

"That's news."

"I need your support. I'll back Liz if you back me."

"You mean you guys haven't decided?"

"No!" he said. "That's what the whole no class speaker shit is about."

"Let me see if I get this right, if Jack can't win, then he'll block the vote. Is that it?"

"In a nutshell."

"You know, Declan? After all the shit we've been through here and that you have personally participated in, there is no way, absolutely no way I can support you."

THE GREAT CANNOLI LOCKOUT   59

"But you can win too."

"Not without selling out."

"Get real. Haven't you been paying attention? This whole thing is about degrees of selling out. When did you get so pure?"

"I don't know, maybe I'm just not dirty enough for this deal."

"Have it your way. This conversation never happened."

Declan stalked off. On my way back to my seat, I walked by Jack, Kirk, Dick, and Aaron at their table and by the Japanese students at another. I waved to Denny, Claude, and a couple of the other Reasonable Guys. I got to my seat with Palmer and Liz. I put her hands over Palmer's ears. "Good god! They can't decide whose dick is big enough to be class speaker. That's why they're voting to block the vote."

Liz and I laughed. Palmer smoothed back his hair. "I heard that and it's true, literally."

I reached for my pie. "What?"

Palmer wadded up his napkin. "The other night I walked into the rec room from my room because they were drunk again and louder than usual. That's when I saw them. They were standing around the rec room kitchen table. Their belts were loose. Their penises were on the table."

Liz and I lifted our napkins to our lips.

"They had a ruler," he said. "They were measuring them."

I dropped my napkin. "My god!"

"Who was it, mate?"

I clutched my napkin. "Do we want to know?"

Palmer pushed his plate back. "I think one was the Texan and another was one of the Japanese students."

I held my napkin with both hands. "I still can't believe this shit."

"I dunno, mate, it's all getting to be a bit surreal. Measuring dicks?! Blimy!"

I wadded up my napkin. "Well if you think that's weird, wait till I tell you what Declan wanted."

"What, mate?"

"He wanted to make a deal. He said he'd back you for class speaker if we backed him."

Palmer took the list. "What did you tell him?"

"I said no of course."

Palmer handed me the list. "Look at this list, maybe we should have talked about it a little."

"Are you kidding? How could we ever trust him to deliver anything, assuming he could?"

"Mate, yeah, he'd have to scab Jack."

"Now, that'd be a hoot. But we need more than his vote to win, and besides, it may be too late."

We looked over to Cleo and Teddy talking to Declan.

The class regrouped the next morning and changed their seats. They were organized by faction. Elise lightly tapped at the lectern. "There has been a request for an election."

Jack's hand went up. "We've already voted. No need for another election."

I faced Jack. "Some of you have voted. We want a secret ballot."

Elise tapped her gavel. "I have made the decision to proceed with this vote."

Jack stood. "Elise, you have no authority over internal class issues."

Jack's crew twisted in their seats.

Elise slammed the gavel. "Let me put it to you this way, Jack. I am the leader of this entire faction, and if you don't like it you can apply for the job when it is open. Right now the job is mine and I will decide what course to take here. Do I make myself clear?"

Jack's pink face turned red, and his fists clenched. Jack's crew turned away from him. Elise looked around the room. No one said a word. She slammed the gavel. "I believe I've made myself clear. The vote will be by secret ballot."

Elise left. Debbie, Liz, Ana, Palmer, and I conferred. Anthony joined us. We took out the lists.

THE GREAT CANNOLI LOCKOUT

Declan walked to the front of the class and stood in front of the lectern. "Can you all just give me a minute? As many of you know, some of us had the opportunity to meet to discuss the problems we have been having in our class. We have felt the greatest sense of solidarity and friendship since we got here. Such that we don't see the need for a class speaker. No one of us is above the rest. We are all equal here. There is no need to distinguish ourselves one from the other and create more division."

I faced Declan.

"That's interesting, Declan, especially since you approached me just yesterday about a deal to back you for class speaker. You said you'd back Liz if we backed you."

Declan ignored me, looked over me to the rest of the class, like I wasn't there, and gave them a pasted-on smile as if I had not spoken.

I walked over to him at the lectern. "As for a sense of solidarity, what about the racist, sexist, and homophobic stuff you've been saying to some of us? And writing on your desk name card every week? And what about the foreign students?"

Declan shrugged. He stood taller to try to look over me as I got closer. "I don't know what you're talking about."

I walked over to Declan's desk and reached for his desk name card. Before I could grab it, Declan nearly ran over to his seat, took the card, and put it under his books. "Sister, it's true that there have been unkind things said to people in this class and for that I am truly sorry."

"Then why don't you let us see what's on your card, Declan. What have you got to hide?"

"Sister, isn't it time now to move away from the pain we've caused each other and move toward healing?"

"Okay. Well, if it's all about peace and solidarity, then why are you still writing shit on your card, even today?"

Declan gathered his books and left.

The next day at noon in the classroom the class voted. Each faction stood by the vote count. One pile yes, the next pile no. The votes were twice tallied, one by one. There was no majority. No winner. The class filed out, lumbering, no one saying a word.

After class we walked home in groups. The Japanese students walked together and spoke Japanese. Liz, Debbie, Ana, and I walked together. Palmer, Denny, Anthony, and Claude walked together. Jack, Declan, Kiernan, and Rick turned into a bar, and Randy and Dennis went with them.

Sandy told me later what followed at the Old English pub. They met amid pool tables, high stools, and sawdust on the floor. Steaks charred. The bar lights dimmed as Jack and the rest got very drunk.

Jack slammed down his pint. "We did it, mates. We nailed 'em to the cross. Did you see their faces? Declan, that was a master stroke."

Declan leaned over the table. "She went for my gut, that bitch. I couldn't believe her."

Kirk laughed and stood to mock Declan. "The greatest of solidarity we've felt since we got here."

Rick raised his glass. "Friendship and solidarity!"

Jack lifted his pint. "I'm surprised you let her get close."

"What was I supposed to do?" Declan said. "Smack her?"

"I guess not, mate. Not in front of everyone!"

Sandy took a slow sip of his beer. "What was on your name card, by the way? Why did she reach for it?"

Declan threw his hands up. "Nothing really."

Jack landed his pint on the table. "No, just your usual jungle-bunny racist stuff."

They laughed, slapped each other on the back, nearly fell over. Sandy took another slow sip of his beer. "You're kidding, right? You don't have all that stuff written down on your name card, do you?"

Declan waved over another pint. "No, of course not. Not verbatim."

THE GREAT CANNOLI LOCKOUT

They laughed louder. Sandy pushed back his beer.

Jack turned to Teddy. "Don't worry, Teddy, he didn't mean Cleo."

Snorting and bent over with laughter, they fell off their barstools.

Kirk pulled up on the table toward Teddy. "He'd never disrespect your woman."

Teddy shrugged. "What are you all talking about? I got a real woman at home. Besides, how many of you have done more than dream about pussy since you got here?"

Dick sat up. "Well, okay, let's see who besides you got any."

Silence. Teddy raised his glass. "I rest my case."

Declan rose. "Well, there's Anthony and the Amazon."

Teddy brushed foam off his whiskers. "I don't think so. Like I said, none of you."

They laughed. Jack got back on his stool. "Aaron get anywhere with Ana yet?"

Kirk filled his glass. "No, not even close. But he's managed to piss all the women off. Oh, and we all managed to get snatches of the teacher until Sandy here made an honorable woman out of her. Right, Sandy?"

Sandy slammed down his empty pint glass. "Jesus Christ. I can't believe you guys. They were right."

Teddy walked over to Sandy. "C'mon now, man. Nobody's trying to besmirch the character of your intended."

Jack stood up, faced Sandy. "Put your dick away, man. We kicked their asses. That's all that matters."

Sandy left. Declan started to go after him. "You didn't need to piss him off."

Jack stopped him. "It's okay, mate. We don't need him anymore."

✳ ✳

In the old church basement, the heater rattled. Huddled in a circle, we knew only each other's first names.

My breath visible in the cold, damp dark, I raised my hand. "I just want to go home. One of my colleagues is being stalked. Every day it's some new kind of assault. I never imagined I'd have to go through this here. It's as if this was all a setup. Like they created an experiment to watch us like rats in a cage, a survival show. Maybe the only reason we were invited here was to amuse the privileged."

When the gathering ended, we hugged and bade each other a day of joy and wisdom. An older woman with silver braids crowning her head pulled me over. She'd been there through the entire saga. She took my hands. "Remember," she said, "whatever they do, they do. What matters is what *you* do, guided by your own values and principles." That's when I knew that no matter what happened out there, in here and in myself I was safe.

10 HARVARD UNION WOMEN

The next morning, I got to class later than usual. Jack, Dick, and Kirk moved to the back of the class. Everyone else had to move around them to find different seats. Debbie, Ana, and Liz waited for me by the door. Debbie took my arm. "Are you okay?"

"Yeah, sure, I'm fine. Why? What's wrong?"

Ana took my other arm. "We didn't see you at breakfast or dinner, so we thought something happened."

"I'm fine." I pulled out a newspaper. "I picked this up. We're in it."

Ana, Debbie, and Liz gathered as I opened it.

"We are?" they asked. "Where?"

I pointed to the article. "Read it."

Liz held up one side of the paper and read. "'Harvard union women lead the revitalized labor movement.'" She turned to me. "Mate, is this a joke?"

"No," I said. "It's about our trip to Lowell."

Denny, Palmer, and Eddie joined us. Eddie bit his lip. "It's true what it says. I've been watching you guys."

I handed off my part of the paper and turned to Eddie. His blue eyes followed my gaze. He moved closer. "I mean, I came here to study. I thought things would get better, but they didn't. I'm sorry I didn't speak up sooner. I've never had the chance to study. I had to work all my life."

66 SCABMUGGERS

The others turned to stare at Eddie. We all slowly made our way to our seats and left him standing by himself.

Izzy came in and stacked books and papers on the lectern. "Okay, now let's move on to the question of labor law reform. Palmer noted yesterday that union density is less than ten percent. Is it the law that's responsible for the forty-year decline?"

Denny raised his hand. "From what I can tell, the legal situation here is abysmal. In the worst of apartheid, we had better labor laws than you do. Here an employer can fire you with impunity. In South Africa, when the Black man had no political rights in society, his union was the source of power and the legitimate vehicle for redress. Here if you're fired, your case can languish for years at a labor board and your union has no political muscle to do anything about it but wait."

Izzy moved around the lectern. "So, is it the law, or weak unions? Or both? Some have argued that the law needs to be amended to make it easier for workers to form internal committees, or works councils. How would that work?"

Claude stood. "In the United States, you don't need a law. You need a revolution!"

We all laughed. *How very French*, I thought. *Like my campaigns back home.* It was always my French members who were ready to strike.

Claude continued, "I am serious. It is not a matter of the law. It is a matter of power."

Izzy walked toward the class. "Touché, Claude, but how do we get there? What about European systems?"

My hand went up. "They have works councils in Europe, but like Claude said, they also have an entire political system to back them up. Labor unions are led by political parties in a parliamentary system based on proportionate vote."

Palmer responded, "Aren't you forgetting something? I mean,

HARVARD UNION WOMEN

even though laws are stacked against us and the progressive leadership got wiped out, isn't there something missing? What about organizing the unorganized?"

"That's easy!" I said. "After the Taft-Hartley wimp-out, they did nothing, and after the Left purges, they cut a deal."

Izzy walked back to the lectern. "Who cut what deal? Since we're intent on veering away from discussing 8a.2, what deal?"

I stood. "The AFL-CIO leadership, who, I might add, were mostly white and male. Capital agreed to support domestic postwar industrial development and the leadership agreed to take what they were offered, even if it only benefited a select, mostly white and male group of American craft workers."

Izzy leaned on the lectern. "Are you saying that some people got cut out?"

"Yes," I said. "Just look around this room. Who has been cut out of the leadership in this very classroom?"

Everyone looked around. Jack stood. "You don't appear to be cut out to me. Besides, what does that have to do with now?"

"Now the deal's off. Taking advantage of globalization and technological changes, capital has taken itself off to more lucrative and easier to exploit markets. The US labor movement has been left high and dry. No strategy. No base. Nothing."

Kirk stood. "Why should we be blamed for taking care of our own?"

Jack raised his fist. "That's right, mates. We had to take care of our own."

Ana's hand was up. She waved it and got up on her chair, then stood on the table. "Are you ever going to call on me?"

The class turned in a wave.

Izzy dropped his cool and pointed to Ana. "Go ahead, Ana."

"Isn't that the question? Who is 'our own'? Aren't we all our own? Aren't we, every one of us, in need of work and food for our families? Is someone in Alabama needier than someone in New York? Is a working man more in need of food for his daughter than her working mother is? The child still needs food, doesn't she? Shouldn't her mother and father both be able to earn the same wage to feed her? The food costs the same no matter who buys it. You don't get a discrimination discount, do you? And why were the sleeping car porters not as important to the AFL-CIO as the brakemen or engineers? Why were the Chinese kept underground, used to build railroads, then excluded or left to die at sea?"

Kirk threw his hands up. "C'mon, Ana, are you saying we shouldn't have tried to at least get something for somebody?"

"No, I'm not."

Jack faced Ana.

"Well, then, what are you saying?"

"I'm just saying that it wasn't enough. It wasn't enough for everybody."

"What did you expect them to do?"

I stood next to Ana. "Fight back, that's what."

"With what?" Jack said. "Their bare hands?"

"With whatever it took."

"It's easy for you to say. You had nothing to lose."

"And now, Jack, neither do you."

Denny stood. "It's almost as if the national leadership trusted capital to take care of its own more than it trusted its own members to fight back. They settled for crumbs for a few."

11 THE PLAQUE

Anthony and I went to see a movie at the Brattle. It was the weekend, and the snow had started to turn to slush—a preemptive melt, a pause, before the next storm arrived. We decided to go early to get back to the dorms before the coming deluge. We got seated, last row, corner left. Our coats, gloves, hats, scarfs off, we settled in. Midway through the movie—I don't remember what it was; I think I've blocked it out—I felt Anthony's hand on mine. *This again*, I thought. I tried to pull my hand away, but he grabbed it and put it on his zippered pants so I could feel his erect penis. I immediately pulled my hand back. I'm not sure I even said anything to him, as it was a full house. I got my things and quickly crossed over people to get to the aisle. I pulled my coat, gloves, hat, and scarf back on and dragged myself out to the street.

I was trying to outpace Anthony while he followed me, when I ran into Debbie and Ana outside the Coop, the Harvard student store. I stopped to compose myself when I saw them. "Ana," I said. "What are you doing here? I thought you were going home this weekend."

"My daughter came to see me on campus."

"You should have told us. We could have—"

"Take a break," Debbie said. "She wants your money, not your time. Ana's been showing me a plaque she wants to give to Elise at graduation from us, since we're not having a class speaker."

"A plaque for Elise? That's a great idea," Anthony said.

69

70   SCABMUGGERS

I stepped toward them. "Who's going to give it to her?"

Debbie put her hand on Ana's muff. "Ana should, of course."

"No, not me," Ana said. "Someone else should."

Anthony tightened his scarf. "How about Liz?"

Debbie folded her arms. "No, that could divide us further."

Ana pulled in her muff. "We'll pick a name out of a hat."

I stepped away. "What if one of those brutes gets to do it?"

Ana pulled her muff tighter. "So be it."

"Whatever, Ana," I said. "It's only days to graduation, and then we can all get the hell out of here."

"I'm collecting money for it. I'll need ten dollars from everyone," she said.

Anthony handed Ana a ten-dollar bill. "Count me in."

I started to walk away. "I'll get back to you, Ana."

As I marched off, Anthony followed me. "Why did you do that?"

"What?"

"Not encourage her."

"To do what? Give Elise some hokey plaque?"

"She's doing something to try to bring us together."

"Don't you get it?" I said. "There is no *us* here."

"Why should they be allowed to set the terms?"

"They shouldn't, but they are."

"Only if we let them."

I dropped my backpack, pulled out a bill, and threw it at him. "Here. Here it is. Take it. Is this all it will take?"

I slung my backpack over my back and walked off in the snow and started to cry. He followed.

"Look, you're upset. This isn't about the plaque, is it?"

I pointed to the theater. "It's about what happened in there."

"Look, I'm sorry. I got carried away. I shouldn't have . . ." Anthony took my hand.

THE PLAQUE   71

I pulled it away. "Don't touch me," I said, as I sobbed and walked aimlessly in layers of snow.

Every piece of ground we had fought for would now be reduced to a ubiquitous plaque. And worse, there was the betrayal I couldn't give full words to that had happened in the theater.

✳ ✳

We gathered the next morning in Radcliffe Hall dining room for coffee and to finalize assignments before class. Ana went from table to table to collect money for the plaque. Eddie approached her. "Ana, I think the plaque is a great idea. Some of the guys have been talking and we've been rethinking things."

Ana stuffed more bills into her fat envelope. "Oh?"

✳ ✳

Palmer, Kenji, and Kenzo got to Ana as she started counting the bills. Palmer led the way and leaned toward Ana.

"Where's Simone? Is Liz here?"

Tens and twenties in her hand, Ana pointed to the coffee kiosk. "They're by the coffee. What's up?"

"Just come over before class," Palmer said.

Rick, Kirk, and Aaron were at the next table, hunched over like something was about to happen. Debbie, Liz, and I balanced our coffee as we gathered our books. The Japanese students talked among themselves.

Palmer joined us. "I think we've found two more votes."

I put my books down. "What?"

Liz put hers down. "It's days to graduation."

Palmer leaned in. "I know, but I've been talking to the Japanese guys and they're willing to vote for Liz this time."

"Why?" I said.

"True to form, Jack's continued to be an asshole. You saw him in class the other day. They've just had it."

"So, what are you talking about, mate, a revote?" Liz asked.

"Yeah, mate," Palmer said. "A revote."

"How's that going to work?" I said.

Ana joined us with a wad of money and started to count it. "Almost enough. What is going on?"

Debbie helped Ana count. "Palmer thinks we have enough for a revote for class speaker."

Ana unfolded more bills. "Really? Sandy and some of the guys have had it with Jack, and they might vote with us this time."

Ana handed me a handful of pennies.

I felt the coins, heavy in my hand. Was this one of the many magic-penny-omen moments I had experienced that signaled a shift? It wasn't just the one or two stray ones I found on the street that affirmed a thought or direction I was about to take. Here was a whole handful. Dialectical materialist as I was, these pennies had meaning to me.

Elise walked in.

Palmer headed to Elise. Liz joined the money count. "My god, mates, I might have to get something ready in four days."

I stacked the pennies. "That's if we can pull it off."

Palmer came to the money count. We all stared. "Well?"

"She'll announce a noon meeting at first break," he said.

The morning lecture ended. Elise walked to the lectern. "Before anyone leaves, I have an announcement. I've had a request to discuss revoting for class speaker."

Jack stood. "We've already decided that."

Elise lifted the gavel. "Apparently, Jack, there has been a change in position on the part of some members of this class."

Jack looked around, staring at the Japanese students.

Elise gaveled. "I don't want a hand vote. But I will honor your request if the majority of you stay in your seats."

THE PLAQUE

73

Jack stormed off; Aaron and Rick followed. Cleo left with Teddy, and then two others left.

Anthony sat at the edge of his seat in need of a bio break. "How long? Some of us do have to go."

Eddie turned to Ana. "I'll stay for a meeting."

Sandy looked over at Eddie. "So will I."

A slim majority of the class stayed in their seats to support a new vote.

Elise gaveled. "A noon meeting here right after second lecture. I'll ask the kitchen staff to delay lunch."

Palmer pounded his desk. "Yes!"

During the morning break, Palmer joined the Japanese students. Liz, Debbie, Ana, and I sat together at our usual table hidden behind the coffee kiosk and could hear Jack and Kirk.

Jack waited for Kirk by the coffee kiosk. Jack took a sip of his coffee. "What happened?"

"Looks like they got the votes."

"How many?"

"I don't know, Jack, but more than half stayed in the room. We're going to vote again right before lunch. Doesn't matter now, does it? You don't have enough time to beat everybody up before lunch." Kirk laughed and started to walk away.

Jack pulled Kirk's arm. "Why did you stay?"

"One thing I've learned about this business is that you've got to know how to count and you always have to leave yourself an out. It's simple, buddy, I bought insurance."

Jack crumpled his empty coffee cup. "We'll see about that."

The second lectured ended. Elise approached the lectern. "There has been a request that I preside over this proceeding, and I have decided to honor the request."

Elise tapped the gavel in her hand.

Jack stepped forward. "With all due respect, Elise, I think we all should have a say in what happens here."

Kirk leaned over to Jack. "I don't think you want to go there again, buddy."

Jack turned to the class. "But we've already voted."

Declan stood. "That's true, Elise. And besides, I believe in order to overturn a majority vote, two-thirds must be willing to overturn the defeated motion."

Aaron pulled out *Robert's Rules of Order*. "It's true, Elise. It's right here. There has to be two-thirds."

I stood. "But it was a tie. There was no majority. We want a secret ballot."

Liz walked over to me. "Wait, mate, I don't think we can count high enough to win at two-thirds."

Debbie walked over. "She's right. At the most, we've added four or five more. We need seven new votes total, plus a solid original base to reach a two-thirds threshold."

Palmer surveyed the room. "Let's get a motion on the floor."

Palmer started to raise his hand. I walked over to him. "No, wait," I said. "We don't have it. We're only going to make it worse for the new people on our side."

"We've got to test it," he said.

"Not without getting them creamed for coming to our side and standing up to Jack."

Elise gaveled the lectern. "Do I hear a motion?"

Palmer raised his hand. "I nominate Liz for class speaker."

Elise gaveled. "There is a motion on the floor. Do I hear a second?"

Palmer looked around. The room was silent. He stared at me. Jack stared at the Japanese students, and they stared back.

Elise gaveled. "Do I hear a second?"

I whispered to Palmer, "We just don't have it now, Palmer. See who seconds you."

Elise gaveled. "Going once, going twice. The motion fails for lack of a second."

THE PLAQUE

75

Palmer stood to face me. "Why didn't you second it?"

"We didn't have two-thirds, and besides, what did you think was going to happen to anyone new who voted with us this time?"

"So, Jack wins again?"

"No, we did."

"Now, how's that?"

"We played our game," I said, "not his."

"So much for fighting back, no matter what it takes."

"There's a difference between fighting back and walking into a slaughter."

"Everybody has a choice to make."

"Individually, maybe, but collectively we can't risk people to prove a point to a bully. We need more time."

Jack raised his hand. "Thank you, Elise. I believe some of us will be absent this afternoon as we will be preparing for tomorrow's presentations. Right, blokes?"

Kirk packed up his books. "The usual place?"

Jack led the way. "The same."

12. LIGHTNING STRUCK THE GARBAGE TRUCK

The next morning, Jim Green stood at the lectern. "Today we'll be wrapping up the presentations you have prepared for the class on your topics. There are several of you, so please keep to your allotted time slot so everyone has enough time to present their work. Simone, I believe you are first up today."

It was my turn to tell a story about a fight to be part of the larger fight for respect and dignity. A story about the most vulnerable workers, garbage workers in the South, who, like their forebears, the contraband soldiers in the Civil War, had to fight for the right to fight. Here, the garbage workers had to fight for the right to be recognized as a union. Lead by T.O. Jones, it was a battle for union recognition.

I took my place at the lectern and laid a small stack of placards face down in front of me. "My topic is the labor movement and the Civil Rights Movement. I am a member of the American Federation of State, County, and Municipal Employees. You may not know that it was Black garbage workers, AFSCME members, in Memphis on strike who Dr. King went to support the night that he was killed. The garbage workers went on strike in Memphis because one of their members was killed, crushed by a garbage truck. Lightning struck the drum of the garbage truck, where the garbage worker and a coworker had taken cover from a storm to eat their lunch. Lightning activated the crusher, and he was crushed to death in the garbage truck."

I started to cry and struggled to compose myself.

LIGHTNING STRUCK THE GARBAGE TRUCK   77

"Much is made of Dr. King's life, work, and tragic death, as it should be. But little is ever said about the many women and men, nameless working people who gave their lives in the fight for respect as human beings and dignity on the job, like the Memphis garbage worker who got crushed to death in a garbage truck. How many others whose names we didn't know rose up and fell? The union went on strike and stopped garbage collection in Memphis because the mayor refused to recognize the union. A rally was organized. The National Guard was called in. They pointed guns at the strikers, their families, and supporters. Unarmed men walked in front of the guns. They wore placards to demonstrate their respect for each other and to affirm their dignity as men. It was the courage of everyday women and men who made this movement. Dr. King knew that and said the following about labor."

The light went off, and a video of Dr. King was shown making a speech about the dignity of work and the right for decent pay. The video depicted men wearing I AM A MAN placards walking single file in front of the National Guard troops who had rifles drawn. I sat down and tried to stifle a sob while the video played. Some of the men and women in the class got red-eyed. The lights went on. I took my notes back to the podium.

"It was the work of Ella Baker, who organized the mass grassroots organization SNCC all through the South, and Bayard Rustin, a Quaker, queer labor activist and community organizer, who built ties between labor and the Civil Rights Movement."

Jim came over. "Simone, I'm sorry, but we're at time."

"Oh, sorry. There's so much more to say. I guess I'll just end by passing these out."

Placards that read I AM A MAN were passed around the room. Ana took one, added "WO" to it, and put it around her neck. I sat down and sobs rolled up in waves within me as I looked around to see the majority of the class wearing the placards. Jack, Rick, and Kirk just sat there.

JUST SAY YES

After lunch, the class reconvened. Ana sat at her desk, tearing and folding small pieces of paper. She wrote on each piece and placed them in a fishbowl.

Debbie came over. "Need help?"

"I'm almost done," Ana said, folding the last piece.

Liz and I walked over to Ana. "Mate, what are you doing?"

Ana mixed up the pieces of paper in the bowl. "I'm going to ask this afternoon's lecturer to pick out the person who is going to present the plaque to Elise at graduation."

I looked away. "Oh."

Debbie went to put her hand in the fishbowl. "It's still secret, right? I mean, Elise doesn't know, does she?"

Ana stopped her. "Thanks, Deb, I got it."

"Mates, as far as I know, Elise hasn't a clue. By the way, I've invited Mindy to join us tonight for a little nightcap," Liz said.

Debbie pushed the fishbowl to Ana. "Really, after what she did? Letting herself get passed around like that?"

Debbie, Ana, and I were working-class Catholics. We were from the end of feminism that held the body as sacred and sex as something private and holy. Very far from another side of feminism that held up a woman's right to decide with who and how to share her body. That she had every right just as a man does to be with or do whatever she pleases. I did and do absolutely support a woman's

JUST SAY YES

agency over her own body. And I held to intimate integrity between two people as they each defined it.

There was also a class issue. The consequences for working-class women were very different. Any dalliance that resulted in a pregnancy could end in a beating, being shunned, shamed, or outcast. In our very Catholic, almost cloistered enclaves, there was no clinic to whisk you off to for a procedure. There was no aunt in another town to take you in. Young women I knew ended up in foster care after their families threw them out. Or, like my own mother, they left school and married despicable men.

Elise entered the classroom with the AFL-CIO women's department director. The properly attired matron was no firebrand. Elise gaveled. "Now, listen up. We're going to hear what the AFL-CIO is doing about issues facing working women."

Ana walked over to the speaker with the fishbowl. "Would you do something for us? It won't take long."

"Sure!"

"Please just pick out a piece of paper."

"Okay."

She picked it out. Ana removed the fishbowl. "Thank you, now please read it."

She opened the folded paper. "Denny Mosime."

Half the class erupted with applause. Jack clenched his fists. Denny's eyes widened as he searched for a response.

I closed my eyes and thumped my chest. "There is a god."

I reached over to Denny and slapped him on the back.

"Congratulations, Denny! You've been selected to present the award."

"I don't know what to say," he said.

I reached to take his hand. "You just have to say yes, Denny! Just say yes!"

"Yes!"

Liz shook his hand too. "That's it, mate. That's it."

14 SHAKE YOUR TAIL FEATHERS

That evening in our doom room, Debbie and I prepared drinks and snacks. Ana and Liz brought photos. We sat around the kitchen table, snacking, drinking, and exchanging photos.

I handed Ana a photo. "Here's a good one of you."

She passed me a photo. "That's a nice one of you."

Liz looked on. "Yes, and here's one of Mindy. She should be here any minute."

Debbie filled her plate with more chips and dip. "I still can't believe she let herself get passed around like that."

"Mate, don't you think you've been a little hard on her?"

I reached for my ginger ale. "Liz, she let us down."

"Yeah, mate, but who did the passing?"

Debbie dipped her chip. "Liz's right, we've been treating her a lot worse than the assholes."

I took another sip of my ginger ale. "But let's get real here. This wasn't just any isolated college, 'let's get drunk and anything goes' situation. Believe me, I know about that firsthand. The truth is, she scabbed us, all right?! These weren't just random guys. These were the very same assholes we've been fighting tooth and nail since we got here. So, to be very clear, I'm cool with 'it's my body and I do what I want with it.' I'm all the way down with that. But that's not what happened here. She defected to the enemy. Plain and simple. She scabbed us."

80

The doorbell rang. Liz got up to get it. She opened the door, and it was Cleo. "Oh, Cleo, what a surprise."

Liz looked around the door to see if anyone else was there.

"It's just me," Cleo said. "I came by myself."

"Oh, I thought Mindy might be here too. Come in. Come in. Hey, you guys, it's Cleo."

I brought another chair to the table. "Hi, Cleo. Liz, you're starting to sound like an American, 'you guys' indeed."

Ana and Debbie laughed. Cleo took a seat. "You all must be surprised to see me."

I sat back down. "Well, sort of."

Cleo unwrapped her scarf. "I've been thinking about coming up for some time. I just wanted to say I'm sorry."

Liz set a plate. "Cleo, you've nothing to be sorry for."

Cleo folded her scarf. "Yes, I do. Let me finish. I need to say this. Then I'll leave."

Ana brought a bottle to the table. "What is it, Cleo?"

"I didn't think you guys cared about me that day you left me a note and didn't wait for me before going to dinner."

Debbie shifted. "We didn't know it was your birthday."

Cleo smoothed her scarf. "I know. How could you know? That doesn't matter now. I let my feelings get out of control."

The doorbell rang. Mindy walked in. "Hi, you guys. It looks like we're having a reunion."

Ana opened the bottle. "Shall we celebrate? I brought this from home, freshly pressed hard cider."

Ana poured. I brought out a large radio. "I finally found a good oldies station. Oh, good, listen to what's on now."

I reached for Liz's hand. Liz put her cider down. "What are we doing?"

"Liz, you're about to learn the Slauson Shuffle." The music played. Cleo and Ana got up, and Debbie and Mindy joined them. Soon we started to line dance.

82 SCABMUGGERS

The song ended and we fell back on the couch, laughing, tipping our glasses. The phone rang. Debbie got up. "Who could that be?"

I poured more ginger ale. "It's probably for you."

Debbie handed me the phone. "It's for you."

"Who is it?"

"It sounds like Sandy."

"Sandy? What does he want?"

I heard Sandy, Palmer, Eddie, Anthony, and Denny all gather around the phone. "Are you guys coming to the party in the rec room?" they asked.

"I'm not," I said.

I held out the phone. "They want to know if we're coming to the rec room."

All the women shook their heads.

"I don't think so," I said. "Bye."

I hung up. It rang again. "So sorry, I don't drink . . . You want to bring champagne up here? Not interested. Bye."

Debbie leaned over. "Aren't you taking this a little too far? I live here too. You don't have to drink any."

Ana recapped the cider. "Yeah, call them back."

"Mate, I don't see why we can't let them bring their champagne up here, stay for a little while, and leave."

I dialed. "Look, Sandy, I'm going to give you a trivia question. If you answer this question correctly, you might have a chance of coming up. Who sang this song?"

I wet my lips. "The 'Johnny Get Angry' song. Call back when you have the answer."

Debbie leaned in. "What's the answer?"

"Beats the hell out of me." We laughed. The phone rang. I pushed the speaker button.

"The Bluebells."

"No, not the Bluebells. Sorry. Try again."

SHAKE YOUR TAIL FEATHERS

I hung up. We laughed louder. The doorbell rang. Palmer, Sandy, Denny, Claude, Eddie, and Anthony crowded the doorway.

Liz put the radio on the table. "Mates, I just learned the Slauson Shuffle." Debbie and Ana rolled up the rug. Jack, Rick, Kirk, Aaron, Teddy, and Declan showed up with wine and beer. The Japanese guys arrived with sake and food. Elise came in, and someone handed her a beer. She got on the dance floor, shook her tail feathers. We drank and danced. Aaron stood in front of the room. "I'm going to show you a Black fraternity stomp."

Aaron hit the floor with his right foot. Then his left. The class all lined up behind him.

"No more oppression."

The class stomped.

"No more bosses."

The class stomped.

"No more fear."

The class stomped.

"No more hate."

The class stomped.

I stepped to the front of the room.

"No more sexism."

The class stomped.

Ana stepped to the front of the room.

"No more racism."

The class stomped.

Debbie stepped to the front of the room.

"No more homophobia."

The class stomped.

Liz stepped to the front of the room.

"No more small-minded men."

The class stomped.

Mindy stepped to the front of the room.

"A lot more uppity women."

The class stomped.

After a series of continued stomps, the dance ended. We engaged in freewheeling dances, circle dances, break dances. Two students swung each other so hard they crashed into a table and chair and broke them. The wild dancing ended. The energy was high. The slow dancing began. Liz danced with Jack. He was brotherly toward her. They did a distinctive Australian two-step. Sandy and Mindy danced together. Teddy and Cleo did a slow grind. Some of us stood on the balcony overlooking the Charles River, and at a distance we could see the Harvard domes lit up beautifully in the night.

Anthony came to me on the balcony. "You've been avoiding me."

"I've been busy getting ready to go home."

"We always managed to find time."

"What is it, Anthony?"

"Look, I'm sorry."

"It's done now," I said.

"Yeah, but it's not the same."

"Let's just leave it alone."

There was nothing left to say to Anthony. Whatever promise of a friendship there had once been between us had been irrevocably broken. There was no going back.

THAT'S NOT HAPPENING HERE

left the balcony and went inside. I saw Dick and Aaron standing next to Kenji. Dick had taken a kitchen towel and stuffed it into Kenji's shirt. "This ought to help you with a little more on top. Do your geisha dance for us one last time."

Dick laughed as he patted the towels in Kenji's shirt. He turned Kenji around, patted him on the butt, and pointed him to the middle of the room. A circle formed. I walked over, took the towel out of Kenji's shirt, and put it back in the closet. Then I went back to where Kenji was standing and faced Aaron and Dick. "That's not happening here."

Dick motioned to Kenji. "He doesn't care."

Kenji left. I looked at Aaron and Dick. "I said, that's not happening here."

Aaron moved closer to me. "You don't run anything here."

"If you don't like it, you can leave."

Dick moved in. I faced them both. "You can both leave."

The class moved in around us. Aaron got within inches of my face. "You can't tell us what to do."

"Like I said. You can leave."

Elise took Aaron aside. "Who does she think she is?"

Their voices trailed off. Aaron left. Dick sat on the couch and sulked. Jack said nothing. The party went on.

Ana left to go to her room across the hall to get more snacks. She

86 SCABMUGGERS

walked in, went to the kitchenette, and picked up the snacks. She turned around to see Aaron standing in the doorway.

"Aaron!"

"The door was open. I hope you don't mind."

"You can't stay."

"I just want some time with you, alone. Just us."

Aaron moved closer. Ana moved away. "If you don't leave now, I'll scream. They are all next door. They'll hear."

"It doesn't have to be like that, does it, Ana? Besides, the music's so loud they won't hear us. Just relax, it'll be okay."

Ana moved toward the door. Aaron put his body against the door as Ana reached for the doorknob. Her right hand on the doorknob, Ana pulled on it. "Move!"

Ana started to scream. With his black gloves, he grabbed the doorknob from her. He pushed her back with the door, nearly knocked her down. Aaron left and ran down the stairs. Ana locked the door, put her back against the wall, slid down to the floor, and sobbed.

I kept looking at the door to see if Ana had come back with the snacks. It was so unlike her to be late with food. I walked across the hall and could hear her though the door. It sounded like she was on the floor. I bent down and knocked. "It's me," I said. She opened the door and slid back down to the floor. I sat on the floor with her and she told me what had just happened.

The next day, I dragged myself through the snow to the decrepit church, made my way down the stairs to the circle of women who met there every morning, The Morning Glories. I took my place in the circle.

"Some days I wake up and can't believe that I am in this prestigious place and that women in my class are fighting every day for simple respect and dignity. That we have become quarries to be hunted. Subordinates to be tamed. Subjected to touches. Ignored by professors. There are no women core faculty members here, much less any faculty of color. It's no wonder some women have given themselves over to be passed around, literally allowed themselves to be manhandled. The other day, a student I trusted took my hand and tried to put it on his penis."

# LEGAL SEA FOODS

The women met at Legal Sea Foods to begin our goodbyes. There were stacks of little boxes and cards in the middle of the table. I looked at the pile. "You guys. You should have told me you were bringing gifts."

Debbie handed me a jewelry box. "These are for you."

I held an earring up to my ear. "They're beautiful!"

I kissed Debbie on the cheek. Liz opened a box. "That should go with this, mate. I got a different one for each of you."

Liz placed a scarf around my neck. I started to cry. Liz continued draping each of the other women with a scarf. I dabbed a napkin to my face. "Oh god, I hate crying. You guys, I have something to tell you."

"Mate, what is it?"

"I haven't been completely honest about why Anthony and I aren't hanging out anymore."

Ana put her gift down and looked up at me. She and Debbie traded glances. Debbie moved her chair closer. "Something happened, didn't it?"

I nodded. Liz moved closer, put her arm around me. "What is it, mate?"

I felt my tears welling up.

"It's all right," she said.

I caught her shooting a worried glance at Debbie and Ana. Ana's eyes widened.

"I told him no, I couldn't," I said.

Ana dropped her folded hands in her lap. "You too?" She reached for me. "It's okay. Why didn't you tell us sooner?"

"I thought I could take care of it myself. I didn't want to add more to what we've been dealing with."

Ana took my hands in hers, held them. "Been there. Done that. But not sharing with us took you away from us. It's like you didn't trust us to hold you up, the way you've been holding us up."

"I know, and I'm sorry." They had trusted me. But I had learned early on not to trust or tell anyone about sexual assault. Telling them was like falling into a hole I couldn't climb out of. Yet my heart broke open in a way I hadn't expected, opening myself to their care, kindness, and acceptance.

"Mate, don't you see that by telling us, instead of adding a burden, you've helped us all share the same burden," Liz said. "It makes us all vulnerable and strong at the same time. Hang on—let's wipe your nose. I'm getting you a new scarf. You've got snot on this one."

A laugh bubbled up, then another. We sat back and laughed, each wearing a different scarf, mine with snot on it.

The next morning, if it were possible to get colder, it did—so cold that the sexton at the ancient church where the Morning Glories met finally turned up the heat. The pipes rattled more loudly. Even so, our breath was visible in the air. Huddled in our circle, I felt freezing ripples moving up and down my skin.

I raised my hand for my last share with the Morning Glories. "I've come to say goodbye. I go home tomorrow, after graduation. I already miss you. Your support and the support of my colleagues have made my stay here bearable. I've learned so much and been changed in ways I don't even know yet. I harbor no illusions about the work I've chosen. The truth of it is sometimes too hard to hold. But knowing it has somehow freed me."

I tightened my scarf. "I know what happens when people band together against any form of tyranny. They connect in a way that can only be described as spiritual. Making a commitment to stand together binds them, yet frees them at the same time. Their common truth is shared and their courage to demand respect and dignity becomes stronger than their fear."

I pulled on my gloves. "That's when they know power—their own and that of others. A shared power."

The Morning Glories made a list of their phone numbers. At the end of the meeting they gave it to me for my journey beyond that room and circled me with hugs and goodbyes.

But for the grace and kindness of these random women, strangers, really, and spiritual warriors in their own right, who struggled every day with challenges to their spiritual, physical, and emotional sobriety, I would have been lost. Saying goodbye to them warmed me with gratitude for having known them.

17
PENNIES EVERYWHERE

Early in the morning on graduation day, I walked by Harvard Yard, looked in the coffee shops, went past the gym, the library, and the dorms to the newspaper kiosk, and waited for the newspaper vendor. I remembered the giddying excitement when I had gotten here, how I had fallen in love with the simple elegance of New England Yankee architecture, style, and charm. Now, how past that delusion I was, yet stronger in a way I hadn't expected, as I had joined a historic sisterhood of rebels, the scabmuggers and the mill girls. Unrecognized and uncelebrated, they were also part of this regional history, more real to me than the pseudonymous John Harvard.

There was a commotion in the square. The newspaper vendor, a middle-aged, balding white man with a thick Boston accent, handed me a *Globe* and a *New York Times*.

"Your usual?"

"Yes, and my last."

"Going home to Seattle, is it?"

"Yeah. What's all the commotion about?"

"It's the weirdest thing. Somebody dropped a whole roll of pennies in the square. They're everywhere."

I paid, grabbed my papers, ran to the square, and stood in the middle of it. Shiny pennies were all over the bricks. I picked one up, then another and another. I kissed a handful of pennies and put them in my purse. The pennies were the promise of hope. The huge display

91

of coins all around me on the bricks was a sign that I was going in the right direction. These were not the single or sometimes double coins that I had followed here and there like breadcrumbs to lead the way, this way or that, never sure if I could trust the direction. Now they surrounded me and I could dance in them.

Before class, I stopped at the cafeteria with my stack of newsprint to get coffee and breakfast. Kenji joined me. I moved my papers over. "I want to personally say goodbye and wish you good luck," he said.

"Thanks. But I'm a little surprised—you guys don't usually come to our table."

"I know. It took too long. I don't know why. We just didn't know what to say."

"I'm sorry we didn't get a chance to talk sooner," I said.

"So am I."

Kenzo and the other Japanese guys joined us. We talked about going home and were finally able to have the conversations that we couldn't have had before about culture and custom. Conversations limited by culture and custom for both of us. We talked about how different their interactions with women were back home. How little they shared with their wives and girlfriends. They also described the formal way Japanese men proposed marriage, and the fact that acceptance was assumed. The women there were so silent that their silence meant yes.

I marveled. "That would never work here." I could see their faces light up in laughter for the first time. The ache of not knowing them deepened.

WHERE IS IT?

Ornate marble pillars held up the arch that framed us as we assembled on the Harvard Law School steps for our group photo. In a departure from the cold, hard winter we'd learned to live with, the air was clear and the sun was out. Clear enough for us to have our photo taken outside. It was like we were in grade school, laughing and teasing while being pushed and pulled this way and that to get us into line one last time. In the front row, Liz, Ana, Debbie, and I wore our gift earrings.

Liz reached back to Palmer. "Well, mate, we've made it."

"That we have, Liz," he said. "I'm on the first flight out of here as soon as graduation is over."

"We're touring the States and will return to Oz in two weeks."

"Liz, this been an extraordinary experience and my great pleasure and honor to know you."

"Indeed, it has. Mine too, mate, in making your acquaintance. You have been an ally in this fight and I will never forget you."

"Nor I you."

The photographer snapped our pictures. We blinked back tears. Picture taking ended and we entered the Harvard Law School auditorium. Chairs were arranged in curved rows in front of the stage. The Harvard Trade Union banner hung in back of the stage. Family and friends arrived; there were introductions, handshakes, and back slapping. Photos were taken in groups of various configurations in front of the banner: the Reasonable Guys, the women, the Reasonable Guys and the women, roommates, etc. The podium on the stage was flanked by seats on each side of it for dignitaries, professors, and presenters. Debbie and I stood with her husband and son, whose South Boston accents amplified by three made it fun.

Ana came running in and ran over to us. She was shaking, almost in tears. Debbie and I each grabbed one of her elbows and pulled her away from Debbie's family.

"Where is it?" Ana said.

Debbie held her shoulders. "What? Where is what? Ana, calm down. What's the matter? Where is it? Where is the award? Elise's plaque?"

I closed in to shield Ana side by side with Debbie. "It's over by your stuff."

I pointed to a chair with her bag and coat on it. "Look, here it is!"

Ana ran over to the plaque, got it, and gave it to Jim Green who was standing at the podium. "Jim, would you do me the honor of holding on to this for me? It's a surprise for Elise."

Jim took the plaque. "I'd be happy to, Ana. I'll just keep it right here behind the podium."

"Thank you, Jim. Please don't let it out of your sight. And don't give it anyone else under any circumstances."

"Okay, I'll just keep it right here behind the podium."

Ana grabbed his hands in hers. "Thank you."

Ana walked back to us, her hands trembling. Liz came. Putting her hand on the back of a chair to hold herself up, Ana sat down, then got up. "Where's Denny? Where is he?"

All I could think was *What the fuck? What now?*

Liz put her hand on Ana's shoulder. "Ana, calm down. Calm down. What's going on?"

Denny walked over to us. "Denny's right here," I said.

WHERE IS IT?

95

Ana hugged Denny and said, "You're here. You're here. You're okay."

Denny pulled a chair close to Ana. "Of course I am. What is it, Ana? Breathe. Speak slowly. Tell us."

Ana's arms were draped around Denny's shoulders. "Okay, okay. It happened this morning on the law school steps. I got here early to help set up. They were waiting for me."

All of us said, "Who?"

"Jack, Kirk, Rick, and Aaron," she said. "I'd already put my stuff down and came out to get something else and Jack stopped me. He said, 'Ana, I know you've worked really hard to get Elise's plaque. We've been thinking that it might be better for one of us to give it to her. What do you think, Ana?'"

Ana took her hands off Denny's shoulders and sat down. "I told him we'd already decided that. I told him you were selected to give Elise the plaque. Then all of them surrounded me." Ana put her hand up to her face. "Jack got this close to my face, pulled my arm, and said, 'Just give it to me now, Ana. Where is it? Just give it to me.'

"I pulled away. 'I will not,' I said. I ran inside and found you guys. Jim Green has it now. He's guarding it."

There was to be no letup in this fight. It would go all the way down to the wire, a fight to the finish.

Denny stood. "Those animals. I cannot believe it."

Liz turned around. "Where are they? I've finally had it."

Ana pulled them back. "No. No. The plaque is safe now."

Debbie and I joined Ana in pulling them back. That was exactly the provocation the assholes would have wanted. Word spread, and the rest of the Reasonable Guys joined the small group around Ana. The music began.

STEP BY STEP

Elise stepped up to the podium. She wore the same beige suit she had worn the day she welcomed us, memorable for its simplicity and convention. "To begin our program, I'd like to welcome Harvard's own Pipettes, an a cappella group of union women and men who carried the union's message to Harvard University. The Pipettes were organized when the AFSCME Harvard Union of Clerical and Technical Workers organized the working women and men of Harvard University. It took seventeen years and these women to show Harvard that 'you can't eat prestige.'"

The Pipettes filed in ascending order in two rows on either side of us up to the stage. As they walked up, they sang. *"Step by step, the longest march can be won."* I locked eyes with them, and a dam of tears broke and flooded down my face. The Pipettes finished singing and took their seats on the stage. Elise turned to the assembled from the podium.

"Welcome to the many guests who have joined us today to witness the passage of this class of the Harvard Trade Union Program. I must say it has been an unusual challenge to direct this program this year. But not one without its rewards."

We laughed.

"There are many dignitaries here to address you, but it is you and only you who can say what your stay here will mean for your work and for your lives in the labor movement. That you have chosen to

STEP BY STEP 97

have no voice today, I hope is not a reflection of what you have to say to the working men and women of this country, and the world, who so desperately need you. I know that many of you have spoken louder by your actions than any podium words can express. You know who you are and I honor you."

Clapping and foot stomping ensued. Professors, dignitaries made addresses. Elise went back to the podium.

"Finally, I hand this podium to Denny Mosime."

Denny walked in a measured pace to the podium, took out his notes, studied them, and put them down in front of him.

"It is my unparalleled privilege to address you today. I come from the mines of South Africa, a Black man, a worker, a representative of workers. In my country, the union was the training ground where the disenfranchised learned to fight for democracy. The union prepared us for the fight for political rights denied to us under apartheid. In political life, we had no voice. In the union, we did. Many of our leaders were killed, exiled, or imprisoned. It was the labor movement that sustained the lives of average working women and men in their daily fight for bread and dignity. The common denominator for each and every battle, defeat, and victory were the common woman and man, who worked with a pick, shovel, and mop in her hand. We did it and we did it together, as we stood on the backs of giants. Giants on whose backs we stood, who supported us, stood by us, took blows and imprisonment, and some ultimately gave their lives. Elise, in the memory of Chris Hani, this award is presented to you as one of those giants who has stood by us, held us up, and seen us through."

Most of the class jumped to their feet, erupting into applause. Elise received the award, wiping tears from her eyes. I wasn't sure what to make of it. Her emotions were genuine to be sure, but I couldn't let go of my belief that she could have done more to intervene, to stop what was happening to us. I had a dawning awareness that this had all been part of a plan. That this whole course had been designed to create an internal conflict to see how we would resolve it. That Elise's role there was not to "fix it"; rather, she was a stand-in for absent "outside protector," the governor, mayor, police, or union bureaucracy that had time and time again in our history failed to act. That any power we had was ours to create, fight for, and preserve.

The students were called up for their diplomas, one by one. The Pipettes rose. *"Lord, take my hand while I run this race. Lord, speak to me while I run this race. 'Cause I don't want to run this race in vain. Race in vain."*

Aaron bowed his head. Ana walked up. The women and Reasonable Guys stood to applaud. Jack walked up to polite applause. Then I walked up, red-faced from crying. Liz stopped me on the way. "Buck up, mate, we did it."

I stifled tears, smiled, waved my diploma. I couldn't hear a thing. It was like I wasn't there, like I was overtaken by some force. The simple seed of resistance that had begun so many weeks before had created a momentum of its own. It had made way for new leaders who carried the fight forward. It had overtaken us all and found its singular expression in resistance that day in a way I could never have imagined. In a small way, we had become a part of the bigger fight that inspired us to dare to act, even if we were outnumbered and fought against the odds like so many who came before us.

Elise handed out the last diploma. "Now please join us in the lobby for a reception following the ceremony."

The Pipettes filed out in song. *"Step by step, the longest march can be won."*

We got up, shook hands, hugged each other. Almost everyone had filed out when Eddie walked over to me. "Simone, can I talk to you?"

"Sure."

"I know this may be too late." His voice cracked. "I had a long talk with Elise last night. I'm sorry I didn't speak up when everything was happening. I just didn't get it until now."

STEP BY STEP

"I don't understand," I said. "Why did you do it? Why did you go along with them? You're a Steelworker."

Tears pooled in his blue eyes. He shook his head. "We took an oath. We took an oath as men."

He was near sobbing. I took his hand, held it, put my arm around him, met his eyes, then turned and walked away.

I had so little else to say to him. Was his manhood so cheaply defined? Was it so easily given away to a tyrant? *Isn't this the moment of working-class solidarity that we fought for and that I idealized? I wondered. Isn't this where the glorious light of worker solidarity shines on workers who walk arm in arm into battle armed with their bare hands to fight the boss?* Yet even with his entreaties, I felt spent. I had brought my whole game to this fight and spent all of the artillery at my disposal. Was there yet some new place for me to go? Some harder, deeper place that I couldn't reach in this moment? Why wasn't this enough? Was there more, a plate of lasagna, some cannoli? A much simpler, more human connection?

The entire class and our family and friends moved to the law school lobby. There was a lavish spread of food and drink. The energy was high. There were more introductions, pictures, hugs, goodbyes. Ana stood in the middle of a staircase. She held up a wineglass and tapped it.

"Can I please have your attention? We have another ceremony to honor our passage here today."

We sat back and watched as Ana led us in a ceremony that she had created. Next to her was a pile of boxes.

"We have had our official recognition," she said. "Now, I'd like to offer our own unofficial but truly inspired recognition. I want to honor the Scabmuggers of this class with the first ever Scabmuggers Solidarity Award. Historically, the Scabmuggers were immigrant women, wogs, as they are now sometimes derisively referred to by some. Italians, like myself, Slavs, Greeks, Irish, Poles, Eastern Europeans. Now they are Latinas, Blacks, Asians."

Her face lit up as she held the room. "The Scabmuggers were turn-of-the-century immigrant union women who patrolled strikes to take out the scabs. They banded together for mutual support. They banded together to do whatever it took to win. In honor of those nameless women, our foremothers in this movement, I want to honor three women in our class today. Debbie, please come up."

Debbie turned to her husband and son, her arms folded in front of her, shrugged in surprise, and walked up.

"Debbie, you've been there through the thick of it. Stalwart sister and friend, arm in arm, shoulder to shoulder."

Ana hugged Debbie. Debbie held up her gift.

"Liz, where is Liz?" Liz walked up. "Liz, thanks for teaching us what international solidarity is truly all about."

Ana handed Liz a gift. She hugged Liz and gave Liz a kiss on the lips. Liz kissed her back to foot-stomping applause. Wasn't that the way of it, though. In the end, Liz got the girl.

"Finally, where is Simone?"

I came up the stairs, frog-eyed from crying.

Ana handed me a gift. "Simone, this is for you." She hugged me. "Thank you for teaching me how to fight," she said.

I held her gift to my chest. "Thank you for teaching me how to win."

I never saw Ana again. On our way home after the ceremony, back across the melting Charles, she gave me a card with a picture of the river on it. In her inscription she wrote: *You are stronger than you think you are.*

In my speculation that the course had been designed and set up like a reality show, I even wondered if Ana was an actual student. If in

STEP BY STEP

fact she was an actor or a plant. Her first name wasn't even Ana; her last name was mysterious. She was gone every weekend. I searched for her over the years but never found her. Why did she stop short of exposing the abuse at the mock arbitration? Did she in fact put Denny Mosime's name on every one of those slips of paper in the fishbowl for the plaque drawing? I will never know.

All these years later, it doesn't matter, as Ana represented the "everywoman" leader I would meet in my career. The organic leader whose instincts about and knowledge of their workplace and co-workers I would come to respect and rely on to win in the battles we fought.

She was the housekeeper who organized an entire hospital precisely because she was everywhere and nowhere. Because she was often poor, Black, or Brown, nobody saw her or suspected her.

It was the same for the kitchen. It was where everybody had to go to exchange information and gather intelligence. And when not required to cook institutional meals, the subversive cooks could actually cook phenomenal food.

She was a big-city meter reader who exposed the city's racist ticketing practices.

She was a social worker who demanded equity for women of color at a national union women's conference.

She was a nurse who inspired entire wall-to-wall hospital staff from housekeeping to pharmacists to strike by saying "Nobody can oppress you without your permission."

She was a clerical worker who dared to complain about her abusive boss and took him to a hearing and won.

She was a closeted lesbian activist who decided to come out after leading a winning campaign to save jobs. One day, she drove to work in a large lavender truck.

There are so many more.

Finally, she was my own OG Mexican American grandmother, a

scabmugger in her own right, who dared to organize her sex-worker sisters in the '40s and '50s to shut down Salt Lake City taverns to run out scabs.

This was her legacy.

ACKNOWLEDGMENTS

I want to acknowledge all my sisters in struggle, past and present.

ABOUT THE AUTHOR

photo credit: Matt Wong

Yvonne Martinez is a retired labor negotiator/organizer. Her work has appeared in literary magazines and on NPR. Her book *Someday Mija, You'll Learn the Difference Between a Whore and a Working Woman,* inspired by her sex worker organizer grandmother, covers her own childhood in Salt Lake City/South Central LA/Boyle Heights and her work as a labor negotiator/organizer in California and the Pacific NW. She is a graduate from the University of Washington, UMass Amherst, and the Harvard Trade Union Program. Yvonne lives in Berkeley, CA.

Looking for your next great read?

We can help!

Visit www.shewritespress.com/next-read
or scan the QR code below for a list
of our recommended titles.

She Writes Press is an award-winning
independent publishing company founded to
serve women writers everywhere.